S0-AIE-450

Acknowledgement

I would like to thank all the usual suspects who have supported me through my writing career and other endeavors.

My family is always number one to me and the addition of my daughter is the most wonderful experience I ever had.

Baby Girl, I will love you unconditionally until my last breath. From now on, daddy will be working diligently for a better future for you and a better society for the rest of the world.

Thanks to my dad for always for showing a lot of enthusiasm about my work. Special thanks go out to all the book clubs and readers who continue to inspire me to get better with each novel. I would like to give a big shout- out to the street vendors and booksellers around the country and all over the world for keeping the world in tune with our literature. Thanks to all the book retailers and distributors who make it possible for our books to reach the people.

A special shout out go to all the New York book vendors and entrepreneurs.

A big shout out go out to my nephews and nieces as well as my brothers and sisters. I would also like to give thanks for being part of the human race.

Last but not least, I would like to thank my fellow writers for making reading fun again for our people.

Introduction

Most of us sometimes dream of being wealthy, as if it would take away all of our problems and stressors. Life is not always about what we carry in our wallets or the number of zeros in our bank accounts. One of the most important aspects of life is being a contributor to society and by that I don't mean that you have to have a great invention or the next billion dollar idea. It's about helping out your fellow man and making sure those around you strive as much as you do.

Being wealthy doesn't take away a terminal illness, it doesn't take away loneliness, it doesn't take away ignorance and it doesn't take away stupidity. However, being a kind hearted and generous person can sometimes lead to a prosperous life even without wealth.

We live in a selfish society where "excess" has been our motto for the last thirty years or so. How many millionaires die and leave their excess life behind abruptly? Many of us seem to have this idea that life ends when we die and that there might even be an after-life. The sooner most of us realize that life never ends the better we will be as a society. Everyone wants to live life to the fullest because we don't want to have any regrets, but what happens to the lives we leave behind? In essence, life never really ends. We really need to reconsider extending the lives of others when we no longer have any more life in us.

Organ donation is one of the most vital necessities in the hood, but we lack donors. We have babies whose lives are cut short everyday because of bone marrow transplant, blood transfusion and kidney failure. My attempt in this novel is to present a situation to the reader where the character's financial wants and needs are fulfilled, but somehow there still remain a void. How can that be if he has wealth? I presented the struggle in Neglected Souls, but what happens after we make it? Do our problems go away?

Never the expert, but I hope I can force my readers to think about some of the issues relevant to the hood and to our growth as a race, community and society. Why is it so hard for some of us to help our fellow man? Shouldn't we want to help make life better for our fellow human beings? Maybe after reading this book some of you will think about it more.

We are not fully to blame because we live in a society where conquest is the key to everything. America has managed to conquer most of the world's resources and position itself as the last standing superpower. And we're brought up to think that our conquest defines our power and strength, but for how long?

Skillful

Back when Jimmy was at U-Mass., he learned a thing or two from the campus skank. There are skanks on every campus across America whose sole purpose is to find the jocks on campus to let it be known that they have a mean head game and they are skillful with the nana. Leslie was that skank, and poor Jimmy was preyed upon during his sophomore year. He and Lisa had decided to take a very brief break from their relationship because it was causing too much stress to her. She worried about the many women who wanted to sleep with Jimmy because he was a star athlete. Jimmy saw their brief break-up as an opportunity to dib and dab in a slew of flavorful available nanas on his campus. Their break-up was only for a semester so she could focus on school, but when Lisa realized that she could lose Jimmy to another prospect, she went back and claimed what was hers to begin with.

Meanwhile, Leslie saw a window of opportunity during a casual conversation with Jimmy when he mentioned that he and his girlfriend decided to take a break from their long-term relationship. The saliva around Leslie's mouth started running like a full open faucet left to run in a kitchen sink, after hearing the news from Jimmy. "What are you doing later tonight?" She asked. "I'll probably study for a couple hours after practice then go to bed around midnight," he answered. Scheming Leslie knew exactly what she was going to do to get a taste of Jimmy's eleven inches that night.

At exactly midnight, she showed up at Jimmy's door wearing a raincoat with a spaghetti thong and spaghetti bra underneath. Leslie was also a breathtaking beauty who was hard to resist. She stood about five feet seven inches tall, weighed one hundred and thirty pounds evenly distributed to the right places with a light complexion. She was considered to be conceited because of her complexion, but her beauty was all real. Her reputation as a head expert preceded her, but don't let her tell it. According to her, only two guys have had the pleasure to get their heads blown by her.

Standing by the door with the coat now open asking, "are you gonna let me in?" Jimmy didn't see any other way, because Leslie was blessed by the creator with curves that are too dangerous to drive on during a snowfall. Her nipples were barely covered by the spaghetti strap holding together what she called a bra, too small for her D cups. And down below, the strap is barely resting on her southern lips and erected clitoris, which forced Jimmy to mum his words like Leon Spinks was his speech pathologist. Leslie had never seen a bulge develop so quickly on a man and she smiled from ear to ear.

Upon stepping into the room, Leslie allowed the rain coat to drop to the floor off her shoulders and without saying a word she got on her knees and went for the gusto. In Jimmy's head, the room started spinning and words like "oh shit, don't stop. Oh God! You're so good," started rolling off his tongue. And Leslie knew that she had that youngen in the palm of her hand. Like most young adults, Jimmy busted a nut less than five minutes after feeling the warmth of Leslie's mouth around his manhood. However, he had more to give and wanted more.

Leslie was directing the whole session and just like an Oscar worthy actor, Jimmy followed his director's orders. She got on his single bed and spread her legs wide open across the bed and pointed to her crotch and ordered him to start eating. Unprofessionally so, Jimmy sat on the floor in front of her and proceeded to suck the hell out of her pussy lips. He almost chewed on them like they were a piece of gum. Leslie had to stop him in his track and slowly showed him how to lick the clit and savor the sweet pinkness spread before him.

Leslie took pleasure in knowing that she was the one shaping this young boy's bedroom skills into a man's. She held back the skin on her clit exposing it to Jimmy and told him to lick it the same way he would lick his favorite ice cream, but slower. Nevertheless, the good student he was, Jimmy had Leslie moaning in no time. She knew that he would lose control early if she straddled him, so she allowed him to enjoy a few strokes from the great view of her round booty because the boy looked like he was in heaven. These sex sessions would go on through the course of a whole semester and by the time Jimmy decided to go back to his girlfriend, Lisa, Leslie was crying and begging because she had become addicted to his long strokes. He was now the lover that she bragged about around campus, not to mention the eleven inch endowment bestowed upon him by the Lord. Jimmy was the man.

However, this night was a different night and it was a different story. Lisa was the beneficiary of Jimmy's polished bedroom skills. He had Leslie to thank for becoming such a great lover. Lisa and Jimmy had just made it home from a fundraising event where Jimmy was honored for his philanthropy efforts in the Boston community. Honestly, Lisa started getting wet from the time the presenter got on stage and mentioned the name of the great honoree whom was her husband. By the time the man was done with his speech about Jimmy, the whole room was in standing ovation for what this great man had achieved. I'm sure if Jimmy read his wife's face correctly he would have noticed the orgasm she reached when he got up to walk towards the podium to receive his award. His speech was classy and brief and everybody applauded him for about one minute, nonstop. He was the type of man that any wife would be proud of and want.

With her wetness still running down her thigh from the night's event, Lisa pulled her husband towards her in the foyer for a long wet kiss when they arrived home. It was the kind of kiss that signaled "my pussy's wet and you better deliver like you never have before." Jimmy had gotten used to it by now and the grin across his face read "fasten your seatbelt and enjoy the ride." Lisa enjoyed that grin and when he picked her up and took her to the family room and laid her down on the bear skin rug, her fire was hotter than a forest fire in L.A in the summer time.

Jimmy threw his jacket to the floor and kicked off his shoes and took off all his clothes as he knelt down to kiss his wife's back. His tongue circled around her shoulders and down to her back as he left light traces of saliva to blow on, causing a little frigid reaction that sent Lisa's nipples to stand at full erected potential, while he unclasped her bra at the same time. He continued down to her ass while palming her breasts in his hands and whispering to her "You know I love you more each day." By the time he came up for air, her underwear was clinched tightly around his mouth and ready to start eating. Not wanting to be selfish, Lisa reached out for his stretched out eleven inch limo of pleasure and started rubbing her fingers on the tip of it.

The sensation of the soothing massage he was receiving at his wife's fingers caused the limo to stretch to its maximum potential and ready to be loaded to capacity. Jimmy extended his elongated body and even more elongated tongue, between his wife's thighs and reached for her clitoris. By now her clitoris was fully exposed like an uncircumcised micro-penis. Jimmy took it in his mouth like he was straighter than straight and Lisa started moaning. Now sitting up to a comfortable position and Jimmy putting in over time between her legs with his tongue, she held on to his head for balance. With each loud moan, he stuck his tongue deeper in her and caressed her clit simultaneously with his mouth. Then came the winding on Jimmy's face and "ooh baby I'm coming. You always make me cum so good with your tongue," Lisa uttered. Not wanting to let her get away from him because of the sensitive nature of her clitoris during climax, Jimmy held her legs tight and forced her to climax multiple times and caused her to shake uncontrollably.

After a taking a moment to regain herself, Lisa saw the big donkey standing before her and all she could think about was riding it. But first, a little oral treatment was in order for the man who had just caused a thunderous vibration to take place between her legs. Palming all eleven inches with both hands, Lisa slowly took the tip of Jimmy's penis in her mouth savoring it like she was partaking in a wine tasting competition. She licked it and took her head back to look at it until she got drunk off of it then stuck the whole thing in her mouth again. Not being able to withstand Lisa's special techniques, Jimmy simply closed his eyes and moaned in pleasure. By the time Lisa straddled him, destination heaven was near. With his hands palming her ass while he lay on his back and she-taking him for the ride of his life, Jimmy's body started a metamorphosis that a grown ass man his size should never succumb to. He was like putty in her hands as she worked her magic on him, causing him to explode and let out a loud roar like a hungry lion that just got fed.

The rhythmic movement of Lisa's ass while he was inside of her continued as Jimmy reached his best orgasm in a long time, but she wanted hers too, again. She grabbed the back of his head and tightened her muscle around the shaft of his penis so he would not lose his erection. A few seconds later the plane was back in the air taking off to Lisa's destination. She tirelessly worked that position until sweat started pouring over her body and his. Recognizing that his wife was working too hard for a nut, Jimmy flipped her over on her back and penetrated her doggy-style because that was her weakness. Before entering, he stuck a couple of fingers in her to check for moisture then took the fingers to his mouth to taste the sweet juices of his wife. After slowly inserting about seven inches inside her, she started begging for more. "Give it all to me, baby," she screamed. She arched her booty up and spread her legs open a little to give him access to her clitoris. While licking his fingers so he could start rubbing her clitoris, he continued to stroke her to the sound of her breath and moans. With each stroke it became more intense and it was a matter of seconds before she reached the promise land.

Sensing that she was about to explode, Jimmy increased his speed to stroke his wife harder and faster so they could climax together. And finally with the gyrating movement of her ass against his sweetest stroke, Lisa and Jimmy both exploded together then fell asleep in each other's arms on the bear skin rug thereafter.

Loving Lisa was always a pleasure for Jimmy, but he couldn't stop thinking about how his mother would react to her if she were still alive. Jimmy would have wanted his mother to love Lisa just as much as he loves her. He even wondered about the rest of the family, if he had a maternal grandmother and grandfather who would spoil the kids that he planned on having with Lisa in the future.

No Future Without A Past

Jimmy and Nina's genetic make-up was a little bleak because their mother, Katrina, had never talked about her family. Katrina held a lot of animosity towards her parents, and she didn't feel that her children needed to know them. After all, her parents had kicked her out of the house when she was just fourteen years old, and they never even tried to look for her. As far as Katrina was concerned, her parents were dead and she no longer considered them family. Of course there were times when she wanted to go back to see her little brother and sister, but the pain that her parents had caused her had forced her to turn her back on her siblings as well.

Since Katrina was hanging on the streets most of her life, she never really had the time to discuss family with her children. The time she spent with Jimmy and Nina was kept to a minimum, and only when she woke them up to get ready for school was she able to talk to them. Nina and Jimmy were so self-sufficient by the age of six; they didn't even need their mother's assistance to get ready for school anymore. Most of the time, Katrina just wanted to stay in bed anyway. Her motherly duties only extended as far as making sure that whatever clothes that her children wore were clean. The last thing she wanted was for the Department of Social Services to be knocking on her door due to the physical neglect of her children.

Although Jimmy and Nina were never told about their grandparents, they both knew that there was a possibility that they existed. They had been told by their teachers at school when they were younger that all children had grandparents. They often wondered what their grandparents looked like, and how grandma and grandpa would have treated them if they were around.

Unfortunately, those thoughts never lasted too long, because they worried about their mother all the time. Jimmy was able to meet his paternal grandparents, however, after he learned that Pastor Jacobs was his biological father. Pastor Jacobs was more than eager to introduce Jimmy to his family as long as his family kept the fact that Jimmy was his son private. The media would have a field day if they ever found out that the Celtics superstar's father was Pastor Jacobs. It would somehow lead to the fact that his mother was a prostitute and a convict. Those investigative reporters knew exactly how to bring about a juicy story that could destroy a black man, especially a well-to-do brother. Jimmy had worked too hard to allow a reporter to destroy his professional basketball career.

Mr. and Mrs. Jacobs had missed the formal years of Jimmy's life and they wanted to make up for it. They fed him like a horse and showed him as much love as possible after they learned of his existence. His grandfather was especially proud because he spent most of his time going to Jimmy's games. The Jacobs also accepted Nina as a granddaughter and spoiled her equally as much. For Jimmy, he had at least found a piece to his family puzzle.

For Nina there were no pieces to the family puzzle. Nina hadn't met a soul from her genealogical tree. As much as she enjoyed being part of Pastor Jacobs' family, she still wanted to meet her own blood relatives. Nina wasn't so much interested in meeting her paternal family members, because she had already accepted Pastor Jacobs as her father figure. She wanted to connect with her mother's family, because she had grown up with her mother. Jimmy was just as curious most of the time, but he didn't let it bother him as much. The fact that they never met any maternal family members was something that Nina and Jimmy had to learn to live with.

A Hunted Past

The only person who ever witnessed the fatal incident between Jimmy and Patrick Ferry in the motel room a few years ago was the comatose prostitute, Jean. Even though Jimmy never intended to kill Mr. Ferry, the crime had been committed, and there was a possibility that he could go to jail if a witness ever came forward. Although the victim's wife, Mrs. Ferry, had decided to call the Boston Police Department to ask them to close the case after she discovered her husband's malicious ways; new evidence could have easily re-opened the case. True, Mr. Ferry's skeletons had been exposed, but Jimmy had no right to play judge or jury and he knew this. Not even the people at the hospital, where Jean was hospitalized, knew that she was connected to the highly publicized murder that took place a couple of years prior.

Jimmy had moved on with his life, and he had been trying his best to repent for his sins by doing more than enough for his community and his family. Deep in his heart, Jimmy knew that what he did for the community was something he would have probably done regardless of the situation. He had let go of the guilt of Patrick Ferry's death, and he filled a void in the community with his services as needed. The secret of what Jimmy had done was between Pastor Jacobs, Jimmy, and Collin.

Since neither Pastor Jacobs nor Jimmy knew that Collin had heard Jimmy's confession to the accidental murder that day; it was believed that the secret only existed between Pastor Jacobs and Jimmy. Collin never hinted that he knew what happened, because he loved his wife too much to jeopardize his relationship with her brother. Besides, Jimmy had become the little brother that Collin always wanted. They spent time together whenever possible, and Collin taught Jimmy a lot during his short life. Collin didn't allow his job as a police officer to interfere with the love for his family.

Jean Murray

Jean Murray, the prostitute witness, had been in a coma for the past two years after she was run down by a drunk driver a block from the police station where she had just been interviewed by Detective Collin Brown. At first, the whole hospital staff thought she would remain comatose indefinitely, but somehow she managed to pull through and regained consciousness a couple of years later. In fact, Jean came out of her coma on the second anniversary of her accident. Everyone at the hospital was shocked that she had finally opened her eyes. She suffered severe head trauma when her body was sent flying fifteen feet into the air when the car hit her.

Jean woke up in the hospital not remembering anything about herself or her life. She could not recall her name, or why she was waking up in a hospital. Amnesia was going to be a new battle that she had to face. Her nurse routinely checked on her to make sure she was still breathing, gave her daily baths, and fed her while Jean was in a coma. Everyone knew that it would have taken a miracle for Jean to wake out the coma, but no one expected for a miracle to really take place. At the time of the accident, Jean suffered a few broken ribs and a broken leg that had healed over the two years. She had no body movement during that time. Jean had to learn to walk all over again.

The hospital staff celebrated Jean's second chance in life by cutting a cake for her. Her doctor was especially happy because he had been very patient with her. The hospital had come close to pulling the plug on Jean, but her doctor had fought to keep her in the hospital because he believed she was strong enough to pull through. The fact that Jean was still breathing when she was brought to the hospital was a miracle in itself. Her doctor truly believed that there was more life left in her.

The recovery road ahead for Jean was not an easy one. She was not originally from Boston, and did not have any family nearby that could help her remember anything about her life. Jean was a run-away teenager who moved to Boston from Delaware when she was just fifteen years old. She got caught up on the streets working as a prostitute in order to survive. When the doctor told Jean that she was brought to the hospital after a near fatal accident, she didn't understand what the hell he was talking about.

The hospital wanted to administer a plan to help Jean regain her memory, but they had no idea where to start. No one had any idea what she was familiar with, and there was absolutely no way for them to find out. Before anything, Jean had to start learning how to walk again. A physical therapist was assigned to her, and she was scheduled to go through physical therapy four times a week in order to expedite her recovery. The state didn't want to pay for Jean's hospital stay any longer, and the hospital wanted to use her bed for other people who needed it.

Jean started making a lot of progress in physical therapy. After a month of therapy, she was starting to take small steps with the help of a walker. She was learning to walk faster, and gaining more strength in her legs while holding onto the rails in therapy. One day while walking the rails, there was a highlight clip of a Celtics basketball game on the television located above her head on the wall in front of her. The game announcer was interviewing the biggest star of the game, and almost instantly Jean remembered hearing a familiar voice. She was startled by the interviewee's voice and fell on her butt. The therapist had to help her back to her feet. The voice brought fear to her and she would have run out of the therapy room if she could.

Jean suddenly recalled the familiar voice telling her "Shut up, bitch!" She couldn't remember when or where the incident occurred, however. The voice scared her to the point where she couldn't listen to it anymore. The therapist took notice of Jean's reaction, and asked if something was wrong. Jean told her that the voice sounded familiar to her, but she couldn't remember where she had heard it.

The hospital took Jean's ability to recognize the athlete's voice as a sign of progress. They wanted to know if she was a Celtics fan or perhaps she had met the Celtics player whose voice she heard. The hospital was quick to point out that the player was quite popular and there was a possibility that Jean could have previously heard his voice on television. For weeks, the hospital tried to help Jean regain her memory, and they got nowhere. Jean, however, was starting to have nightmares and the phrase "Shut up, bitch!" kept echoing in her head. Jean didn't even remember that she used to be a prostitute. She seemed like a lost child and there was no one to identify her.

Jean had completely forgotten about the accident that almost took her life. She keyed in on the incident where someone was killed in a motel room while she was there. She kept thinking about being tied up and helpless while someone was killing the man who had paid to tie her up. After a while, she felt she was losing her mind over something that probably had no significance. She decided to let her memory come back to her slowly instead of trying to force it.

Jimmy's New Life

Jimmy had been playing for the Celtics for a couple of years as a starting forward. He had become the same star-caliber player that he was in college. The community as a whole loved him, and he was involved with many different community groups and organizations. Jimmy and his wife Lisa started a Turkey Give-Away for Thanksgiving during his rookie season, and it became an annual tradition. They also started a Toy for Kids program during the Christmas Season that drew support from many of the local businesses and people from the community.

Life for Jimmy and Lisa was on the upside and they were happy as a couple. They wanted to delay starting a family, because Lisa wanted to spend as much time with her husband as possible before sharing the house with any children. Jimmy was involved enough with the community and the children, that he didn't mind waiting. He also had access to his nephew Collin Jr. better known as CJ to the family, and his niece, Katrina, when he felt like acting like a parent. During the off-season, the kids spent a lot of time at their uncle's house. Jimmy and Lisa spoiled their niece and nephew, and they loved being around them. It also gave Lisa great practice for when she would have her own children in the future. Lisa was great with the children and she didn't mind watching them when Collin and Nina needed to spend quality time together.

Lisa and Jimmy couldn't be happier as a couple, and they shared their happiness with as many people as they could. Jimmy always made time for his fans, and he was never too busy to honor a request for an autograph. He was also fast becoming the leader of his team, and his coach took notice. The following fall when Jimmy returned to camp for the pre-season, he was named co-captain. It was well deserved, because he had demonstrated his leadership qualities on and off the court.

The Celtics' pre-season was off to a great start as they were unbeaten for their first five games. Jimmy took over the lead scoring role that year, averaging twenty-seven points a game along with ten rebounds, two steals, two blocked shots, and seven assists. He had become the all-around player that his coach knew he could be. Jimmy was the focus of every team's defenses around the league. Coaches designed their game plan around Jimmy when they faced the Celtics, and that left his teammates open most of the time for open shot opportunities.

At the end of the pre-season that year, the Celtics lost only one game, and the experts were predicting that they might win the Eastern conference come June. The whole City of Boston was hyped and looking forward to a great season. Most of the Celtics' home games were sold out by early October. Even father Jacobs was having a hard time getting tickets for his kids at the community center. He had to create more stringent requirements for the kids to earn tickets to the games. The kids had to work harder in school, and participate more in their after-school activities in order to be considered for attendance at the games. Good behavior also ranked high on Pastor Jacobs' list for anyone who wanted to attend a Celtics' game with him. The fact that the Celtics had a winning record worked to the advantage of every fan and everyone involved.

The Celtics hadn't been to the Eastern Finals in about ten years, and they were determined to make it that year. The coach relied more on Jimmy who was his star player, but he also placed a lot of responsibilities on the supporting cast as well. The point guard on the team was the second leading scorer, and his favorite target was Jimmy. He had built enough confidence in Jimmy in clutch situations, and that made it easy for him to break down defenses to get open shots for Jimmy.

Jimmy was always the first one to show up at practice, and he was always the last one to leave. Though he was a well-rounded player, Jimmy was never satisfied with his defense. He wanted to improve his defense against the quicker forwards and the guards in the league. He asked his coach to set up special drills for him so he could work on his defense after practice. The more Jimmy dedicated himself to improving his game, the harder the other teams had to work to guard him. He made it almost impossible for any player to score more than fifteen points against him in a game.

Players around the league knew that they were going to have a hard time when they had to face Jimmy. There were a few cocky rookies who did not want to show their respect before going against Jimmy, but after he burned a few of them for forty plus points they started to recognize his prowess on the court. Jimmy was not a vocal leader. He allowed his game and his work ethics to do the talking. He encouraged his teammates to look beyond what was being said in the media, so that they could focus on their game. The media was trying to make a superstar out of Jimmy, but he also knew that they would also delight in his destruction if that should ever happen. Thus, he didn't take the stories written in the papers to heart.

Jimmy didn't care about personal accolades. He knew when he stepped on the basketball court it was his job to perform at the highest level, and he gave one hundred and fifty percent every time. He was admired by the whole Celtics organization, from the owner and the president to the janitors. Jimmy was cordial to everyone, and he would always lend an ear to anyone who needed to talk. It could have been a front that Jimmy decided to change to be a much better person and philanthropist because he evaded jail, but there was something sincere about his way of life. He wasn't doing it just because; it had also become a part of him.

Making a New friend

Jimmy would leave the gym sometimes when nobody but the janitor was around. Every night at the end of practice, he would spend another thirty minutes talking to the janitor about anything and everything. Jimmy and the janitor developed a friendship where they were very honest with each other, and discussed everything in their lives. The janitor was like everyone else who came in contact with Jimmy, he was blown away by Jimmy's kind heart and gentle attitude.

The janitor had become a recluse after a tragedy took place in his family, and he was not comfortable talking to people. Somehow the guy was able to open up to Jimmy and they became pretty good friends. He would tell Jimmy about his upbringing in Hyde Park, how his parents were very religious, how they drove one of his sisters away from home, and another sister had been missing for years and was believed to be dead. The janitor harbored a lot of ill feelings towards his parents, but Jimmy never wanted to butt in. He only listened to the man. Jimmy didn't want to pass judgment or offer any solutions. Most of the time, the janitor was just looking to vent his frustrations. Although the Janitor knew Jimmy's name, Jimmy one day realized that he had never formally introduced himself to the janitor. The janitor felt a little special when Jimmy extended his hand to ask his name at the end of one of their conversations. He told Jimmy that his name was Eddy, and Jimmy introduced himself as if they were meeting for the first time.

Over time, Jimmy learned that Eddy was a bright student who was headed to Northeastern University at one point, but he had decided to forgo school after his sister went missing. He also complained that people saw him as

27

nothing more than a janitor, and he didn't feel like being bothered with people. He lived in a one-bedroom basement apartment in his parents' house, and he had no friends. Jimmy invited Eddy out to dinner one night, just so they could hang out as friends instead of a basketball player and a janitor. They went to a restaurant where Jimmy knew that people wouldn't recognize him as easily, and they had a good time talking through dinner.

The more Jimmy talked to Eddy, the more he realized they had a lot in common. He felt that Eddy was a true friend who didn't like him just because he was Jimmy, the basketball star. Eddy was about eleven years older than Jimmy, but he looked a lot older because of all the stressors in his life. After a period of time, Jimmy started to find talking to Eddy therapeutic, and he started to look forward to their little talks more and more. Jimmy was as normal with Eddy as he had ever been with his own sister and Pastor Jacob. He never really had any friends except for his brother-in-law, Collin. His teammates were more like colleagues than anything. Jimmy cherished his friendship with Eddy. He wanted to reach out to Eddy during his times of need and Eddy was grateful. And that's how they became great friends.

Negotiating the Right Contract

Jimmy had signed a three-year contract with the Celtics when he was first drafted and the Celtics had the option to renegotiate with Jimmy for a long-term deal before his contract expired. The Celtics knew that if Jimmy tested the free agent market they would lose him as a player. Jimmy was already a well-rounded player in only his second year and the whole league knew that he would only get better. Jimmy wanted what was due to him and what was fair to both sides.

Jimmy never wanted anything more than to remain a Celtic his entire career. He was involved in enough organizations in Boston and the rest of the surrounding communities to confirm that he wanted to stay in Boston. As a superstar player, Jimmy could've easily shopped for the maximum salary around the league, and there were plenty of teams willing to pay him top dollars for his services. But it wasn't all about the money with him. It was about establishing something and following through with it. He was already too involved in too many things in Boston to turn his back on the city and the Celtics organization knew that.

At first, the Celtics attempted to insult Jimmy with an offer of ninety million dollars over ten years. The offer was laughable at best. His agent didn't even bother with a counter offer. The Celtics also knew that Jimmy was on his way to an all-star season, and the longer they waited the harder it would be for them to bargain. There were rumors circulating in the media that Jimmy could very well be the highest paid player ever if he went to the right team and those rumors were all over the news. There were teams willing to pay him as much as one hundred and seventy five million dollars for a ten-year contract and

Jimmy knew this. Jimmy knew that he could always maximize his earnings by going to another team, but he wanted to remain a Celtic. Boston was his roots, and he could do a lot more for the city's minority community. The young kids in Boston could identify with him.

Moving to another city to play for a different team was totally out of the question for Jimmy, but he also wasn't going to allow the Celtics to take advantage of him either. Jimmy wanted what was fair to him, and nothing more. He was one of the top ten scorers in the league, top ten in rebound, top ten in assists and steals. Most players with those stats were earning about fifteen million dollars a year or more. The Celtics tried to use all kinds of excuses to try to turn the fans against their star player, but the people had already fallen in love with Jimmy as a person and a player and they wanted him to stay.

Celtics management has always had a problem holding on to great African American players in Boston ever since the departure of Larry Bird, Kevin McHale, Robert Parish and Dennis Johnson. That has also been one of the reasons that they have not made it to the eastern finals in almost ten years. Their last hope of making it to the finals was when the great Reggie Lewis was around and they acquired him for cheap money. Jimmy however, was a different story. Those old ways of maneuvering around a contract were not going to work with Jimmy. His feisty and determined agent made sure of it. The days of finding a new white boy to replace Larry Bird were over. He will always remain the greatest white guy who ever set foot on the parquet floor, but not the greatest player.

In the midst of all the craziness that was going on, Jimmy talked to Pastor Jacobs about what he wanted to do, and Pastor Jacobs advised him to stay focused on his game

and try to improve as much as he could as a well-rounded player. Pastor Jacobs knew that there was really nothing that Jimmy could do except play his best basketball to force the Celtics to cough up the money. He knew that he had to stay focused, but he was worried about going to another team. Jimmy had gotten used to the system in Boston, being the star of the team and he got along with his coach. There was a lot at stake for him, too. Pastor Jacobs explained to him that basketball is not just a sport, it is also a business and
Jimmy had to get used to it.

The deadline to sign Jimmy to a long-term contract was fast approaching, and the Celtics was a playoff-bound team. Jimmy was having a great season, and the Fleet center was sold out for every home game. Celtics Pride was at an all-time high in New England. Jimmy brought back the old Celtics tradition of winning to the city of Boston. The days of sub par records were long gone. People were once again discussing the Celtics by the water cooler on Monday mornings at work. Jimmy made the highlight reel almost every night the Celtics played, and each time was more spectacular then the last. No one was saying that the torch had been passed from Michael Jordan to Jimmy Johnson, but the experts had their hopes up for the future.

The final day to keep Jimmy as a Celtics for the rest of his career was near, and Jimmy's agent didn't want to entertain any offer below one hundred and fifty million dollars over ten years. The Celtics knew that Jimmy was worth every penny, and they also knew that he could get more from another team. The Celtics' first offer was a total insult to Jimmy's game and pride as a player. It was downright humiliating for them to even offer what they did to begin with. Even the experts thought it was a slap in the face for such a great player.

With about five teams with offers topping one hundred and ninety million dollars, the Celtics thought it would be best to lock Jimmy into a contract for one hundred and seventy million dollars over a ten year period. It was announced at a press conference that he would remain a Celtics for the long future. Both sides were happy and Pastor Jacobs reminded Jimmy not to take what the Celtics did personally because it was the nature of the beast.

Jimmy's stock had risen not just in the league, but also in the world of sports period. His number thirty-one jersey was the number one selling jersey in league history during his second year. Nike had signed him to an eighty million dollar long-term contract with his own exclusive line of sneakers. All the other advertisers started pouring in to cash in on Jimmy's celebrity and popularity. Jimmy was hawking close to ten different products and was earning millions of dollars a year. But more importantly, he was one of the best players, persons, and athletes in the world.

Holding His Ground

Everyone close to Jimmy benefited from his newfound wealth, and he was a kind-hearted person who went the extra mile to help the less fortunate. Whenever there was a cause that needed help whether financial or otherwise, Jimmy was called upon because he was always willing to help. Sometimes, he found it difficult to turn anybody down for help. It was getting to the point where Jimmy couldn't spend anytime with his family. Everyone made every event or cause sound more important than the last one. It was starting to take a toll on Jimmy, and his family recognized that some people were trying to take advantage of him.

Pastor Jacobs had a talk with Jimmy, and he thought that perhaps Jimmy should hire a publicist or a manager. Jimmy needed to have a person in his corner who could say no to these people every once in a while. Jimmy didn't know how to go about hiring a publicist or a manager, so he asked Pastor Jacobs to become his manager. After all, Pastor Jacobs was one of the few people who had his best interests at heart. Pastor Jacobs didn't hesitate to accept Jimmy's offer, however, he wanted everything to be done professionally and legally. A contract and salary of one hundred thousand dollars a year was negotiated between them and Pastor Jacobs became the official manager.

Handling Jimmy's entire day-to-day tasks was something that Pastor Jacobs was used to. He had been doing it unofficially for the past couple of years without an official title. Jimmy had always made sure that he was taken care of financially. There was no salary, but Pastor Jacobs received a lump sum amount of money from Jimmy. He was just happy to be a part of his son's life.

Jimmy gave Pastor Jacobs many reasons to be proud, and he was grateful to Jimmy for allowing him to be part of it. The fact that Pastor Jacobs had missed out on the first fourteen years of Jimmy's life was no longer an issue. They had put everything behind them and buried the hatchet.

Jimmy was careful not to mention the fact that Pastor Jacobs was his dad in public. He only shared that information with Nina who he'd sworn to secrecy. He told Nina to not even tell her husband Collin about it. There would be too much scrutiny and scandal if the press ever found out that Pastor Jacobs had fathered Jimmy while sleeping with his prostitute mother. Pastor Jacobs was the only person who could make sure that Jimmy didn't overextend himself to please everybody all the time and he was very tactful with people when dealing with them.

Jealousy and Envy

A couple of weeks after Jimmy signed his big contract with the Boston Celtics, he started getting the cold shoulder from some of his teammates. A couple of the veteran players were especially angry that this young player was able to come in and command such a high salary. Most of them were acting out of anger, jealousy, and envy. If they had taken the time to look at where Jimmy had brought the team, they would've understood why his salary was justified.

All the hard work that Jimmy had put forth to bring his team to playoff caliber status, was being questioned. Some of the players started to refer to him as soft, and Jimmy just allowed their words to roll off his back. The coach sensed the tension almost immediately and he called a team meeting to sort out the disagreements. He noticed that players weren't passing the ball to Jimmy as much and they weren't creating as many opportunities for him anymore. There was one incident where one of the players should have set a pick for Jimmy, but instead he allowed the player to collide into Jimmy which resulted in a concussion. The incident was addressed, and the coach made sure he informed the team about their new franchise player and captain in Jimmy.

Jimmy had become a cash cow, not just because of his plays on the court, but also because he had an infectious personality that people adored. His demeanor on and off the court was always pleasant and he had set very high standards for himself. Jimmy knew that he came from the gutter and he had been given a second chance. He wanted to take that opportunity to help make positive changes in himself, the world, and his community. He didn't take too many things personally, and he tried his best to avoid letting the negative criticism of his game get to him.

The Celtics coach understood that Jimmy was a special player, and he led by example on the court and off the court. Jimmy didn't really allow people to make him reach his breaking point and his teammates tested his will many times. He knew that he was probably the toughest guy on the team, but he didn't have to show it. He would however, occasionally foul some of his teammates harder than he should in practice just to let them know that he wasn't going to let them walk all over him. No blows were ever thrown amongst the players, but the tension was high and the team was starting to lose focus. The Celtics had won quite a few games that season, and their losing streaks never went beyond the two game mark.

The coach noticed that his players sometimes ignored his game plans around Jimmy and the Celtics were on a three game losing streak. He couldn't believe how some of the players were allowing their own selfish anger and jealousy to get the best of them as a team. The coach felt it was necessary for Jimmy to address the team as its captain, and put to rest once and for all the disagreements amongst them.

At the team meeting the coach informed the players that he was meeting with them to sort out the animosity they had towards Jimmy, and he wanted to go back to playing great basketball as a unit. In addition, he told the team that Jimmy would address them toward the end of the meeting. Everyone was to give their full attention to Jimmy and whatever problem they had with him needed to be discussed only at the meeting.

The coach went through the formalities of pointing out what the team had not been doing well on the court, because they hadn't been playing as a team. Through videotape footage of previous games, he pointed out how Jimmy was open on many occasions and he was overlooked by certain teammates. He also pointed out that the defense wasn't helping out when necessary. The coach pointed out all the selfish reasons why the team had a three game losing streak. Some of the players acknowledged their mistakes and vowed to get back to their previous forms and play as a team.

At the end of the meeting, the coach turned the floor to Jimmy so he could address the players as the team captain. Jimmy had a lot to say. "First of all, I would like to address the fact that some of you are angry or jealous of me because of my new contract. I come in here everyday almost an hour before any of you of, and I leave an hour after every one of you. I dedicate a lot of time to perfecting my skills as a player, thus I'm rewarded. If you have a problem with your salary, talk to your agent and don't look at mine. Any player who has problems with me personally should act like a man and come to me to discuss it. I know some of you may take my kindness as softness, but I'm here to tell you that you don't want to test me. We're grown ass men and I shouldn't be hearing about any gripes through the rumor mill. I work twice as hard as everyone on this team to elevate my game to a level that has received recognition throughout the league, so I expect to be rewarded for it. I want to be a motivator that would provoke you into action, not to challenge your abilities."

Jimmy was very sincere and straightforward with the team as he told them that he would give up all the personal accolades and the money just to win a championship with his team. Jimmy was also cautious not to allow his teammates to think that he was soft by pouring out his heart to them. He told every single one of them that if they ever felt that they were tough enough and wanted a chance at him, he would be up to it as long as it stayed in-house. It wasn't a physical challenge, but he told them that he could deal on that level as well.

At the end of Jimmy's soliloquy, some players had their heads down and others took his words as positive reinforcement for the team. The questionable players knew that Jimmy wasn't the type of guy to let down his teammates. Jimmy understood that it was human nature for them to be a little upset over his big contract; however, he also knew that they all had the same opportunities to raise their stocks in the game as he did. Most players are rewarded for their efforts on the court and how well they want to be rewarded is ultimately up to them. The old saying "No pain, no gain" not only applies in sport, but it also applies in life, Jimmy told them.

Nina and Collin

Collin and Nina had stopped seeing their therapist shortly after their second child was born. Collin had been a very loving and supportive husband, and Nina had opened up to him in more ways than one. He was very pleasantly surprised when he came home one day and found his wife wearing a nice negligee with soft music and candlelight throughout the house. Nina had also prepared a nice meal, because she knew that her husband would be hungry when he got home. While Nina's gesture was very nice, Collin wanted a meal of a different kind. He was watching Nina's nice round booty strut to the kitchen in front of him, and he developed a different kind of appetite.

He didn't wait a minute longer to pull his wife towards him as he spun her around to surprise her with a long passionate kiss. As Collin kissed Nina, her body started to shiver as she threw her arms around him to hold on. Collin's hands found their way down to her ass and started gently fondling her until she could stand it no more. Moments later, Nina found herself on the kitchen table with her negligee on the floor instead of at the dining room table where she had planned to have dinner with her husband.

Collin had a way with his tongue, and Nina had never passed up on the opportunity to get a good tongue lashing from her husband. While she was lying on the kitchen table on her back, Collin spread her legs open and started licking her slowly. With every stroke of his tongue she became wetter, and he simultaneously tried to double her pleasure by caressing her breasts with his hands. Collin seemed almost ambidextrous as he caressed his wife's breasts and unleashed the same amount of sensation in both breasts, like Michael Jordan switching hands on his way to the hoop to make a buzzer beater. Only in this moment there was no buzzer to beat, and both he and Nina were going to win no matter what because he made sure it was a win-win situation.

Collin continued to lick the tip of Nina's clit slowly and sensually until he felt her convulsions and her legs tightened around his head and the only words she could utter to her husband were "I love when you eat me, baby. I love you. Don't stop." While his mouth was busy pleasing her, he found just enough time to tell her "I love you too, honey." when he came up for air.

Collin made his way up to her breasts and started suckling on them very gently. He knew that she enjoyed it through the perkiness and the erectness of her nipples. Even after bearing two children, Nina's breasts never lost their form, and Collin was more than grateful. After continually caressing his wife's breasts and rubbing her clit with his right hand, Nina could take it no more and demanded that Collin take her on the table. He dropped his pants to the floor and inserted his ten inch manhood inside of her, and started to stroke her until sweat started pouring all over them.

The sweet moaning sounds of Nina's voice only fueled his passion to please her, and with every stroke he looked into her eyes to see the ecstasy he was unloading on her. After stroking and pleasing Nina while on her back with her legs resting on his shoulders for fifteen minutes, Collin wanted to feel her round booty against his crotch while he penetrated her from behind. He brought her down to the floor and had her lean against the table as he penetrated her from behind. He started stroking her until he exploded inside of her. At the end of their session,

Collin could only say "thank you" to his wife, because she had helped him release the stress from a long day's work. Collin spent the evening in bed with his wife after dinner and they talked most of the night away.

 The therapy sessions had really helped Collin and his wife lead a normal life. Their children were their first priority and Collin made sure that he put his family first. Their three year-old son, Collin Jr. looks just like his dad. Their daughter Katrina favors her mother more. Two year-old Katrina has her mother's personality as well as her physical traits. She's a little star in her own right in their household.

Since Nina and Collin's family grew to four, their lifestyle had also changed. Finding time to be with each other intimately had become a task in itself, because the kids were always screaming for attention. Whenever Collin's parents offered to take the children for a night, Nina never thought twice about bringing them over. Collin was transferred to a different precinct after his promotion to lieutenant. However, Nina had not had it so easy with the police department. Although she was promoted to sergeant a few years after becoming an officer, she was also demoted a year later and suspended with pay. The department claimed that Nina was not making enough arrests and did not issue enough tickets. Even though the Boston Police Department was quick to deny that they had a quota system when it came to arrests and tickets in the hood, it was clearly evident that they did when Nina was suspended for lack thereof.

Since Nina's suspension, she had devoted all her time to raising her children. Although Nina enjoyed being home with the kids, she still hired an attorney to file a lawsuit against the Boston Police Department for their unfair treatment of her. Nina was suspended indefinitely until an investigation into her case was finalized. She was hoping that she could get back to work when the kids became old enough to attend school.

Collin's parents tried as much as they could to get involved in the lives of their grandchildren, however, they spent a lot of their time visiting casinos and playing bingo on the weekends. On a few occasions when the young couple needed quality time together on the weekends, Collin or Nina would drop the kids off at his parents' house. The grandparents were always happy to have the children over, but they were spoiling the kids in ways that Nina didn't approve. The children were able to do as they pleased when they were over their grandparents' house and when they came back home to Nina, she always had a hard time enforcing discipline. She felt that every time the kids spent time at Collin's parents' house it was detrimental to their behaviors.

Nina loved the Browns, but she didn't know how to tell her husband that they were spoiling the kids. Collin himself was spoiled by his parents as a kid, and he didn't see anything wrong with the way his parents treated his kids. Nina didn't know how to tell her husband that she didn't approve of the way his parents treated the kids without offending him. Collin always bragged about how great a job his parents did raising him, and telling her husband that she didn't approve of it would be the ultimate blow.

Like most couples, Nina and Collin had their little feuds too. Because Nina wasn't raised by her parents, it was hard for her to grasp some of the things that Collin allowed the kids to get away with. Collin was not as strict a disciplinarian as Nina would have liked. She felt that the kids took advantage of his soft handle on them when he came home from work. Nina would work hard during the day to establish rules such as nap time, play time, reading hour, and snack time with the children, but when their dad came home he would mess up the whole structure. Nina definitely had a problem with that.

Nina kept a tight grip on her kids because of her past experiences. She grew up without much and she had to work hard to get everything she needed or wanted in life. She wanted her kids to understand that sometimes it would take a lot of hard work to get what they wanted. She didn't harbor any resentment towards Collin for having been raised by his parents, but she felt that he took for granted what she didn't have as a child. Collin and Nina tried to keep the lines of communication open between them when it came to their family. When Nina started to explain to Collin the kind of life that she had led, he was impressed with her tenacity, will, and drive. He promised to always support her when it came to disciplining the children in the future.

Collin never realized how lucky he was in life until he met his wife. It was normal for him to have a mother and a father in his household when he was a kid. So, he didn't see anything wrong with spoiling his own children every now and then. Collin was very appreciative of Nina's experience, but he also had to teach her that their job as parents was to make it easier for their children to achieve their goals in life. He didn't want them to go through all the red tape that he went through to get things done. He wanted to help open doors for them.

There was always middle ground with Nina and Collin. It was understood that Nina was the disciplinarian in the house. Collin was especially soft on his daughter. She was his little girl and there was nothing that she could do wrong in his eyes. Nina wanted to make sure that their children knew right from wrong from an early age. She never had anyone tell her what was right or wrong. She figured out most of it on her own by watching her mother do the wrong thing most of the time. Nina understood that just because she now had a middleclass family, it did not shield them from the harsh reality of the streets. She wanted to have a hold on her kids very early on.

Eddy

Eddy was living in his parents' basement at the age of thirty-two and he never wanted to be much of anything. He was satisfied with his job as a janitor at the Fleet Center. Eddy had no motivation in life. He grew up in a very religious setting, but his household was faced with many adversities. Eddy's parents were faithful Christians who truly believed that the Lord had an answer for everything. Sometimes, instead of resolving their own issues, they prayed for an answer from above. It got to the point where Eddy didn't understand why his parents were so devoted to religion and neglecting the real problems they had at home.

His father, Buck Johnson, had tried to raise Eddy and his two sisters to respect other people and to always put God first in their lives. And Eddy was quite religious himself as a youngster. He attended church three times a week with his parents as a youngster and he was involved in the youth ministry. Eddy truly believed that his parents were setting the right path for him and his siblings. However, they didn't always resolve their issues with common sense. Eddy felt that they had placed too much of their responsibilities in the hands of God, which is a common mistake that many Christians make. Buck Johnson never realized that he had to help himself in order for the Lord to help him.

Every problem that Eddy's family faced was dealt with in the church and through prayer. Sometimes, they really needed more than prayer to solve their problems. In one particular case when Eddy's mother, Mrs. Esther Johnson, was diagnosed with a brain tumor, Mr. Johnson was almost adamant that the Lord was the only cure for his wife. He prayed and prayed, but the tumor just got bigger and bigger. His pastor reinforced his beliefs by holding special vigils for his wife each week. It was Eddy who finally stood up against his dad, and suggested that his mother had an operation to remove the tumor. It was just as well because if Esther had waited another day, the doctor said she would have died.

Buck was hard-headed that way, and it was often hard to convince him that doctors sometimes can perform their own miracles in the operating room. The only person closer to the Lord than Buck was his ignorant pastor who had everyone in his church under his spell along with his wife.

As Eddie got older, he became distant from the church and that created a wedge between him and his dad. Eddy was trying his best to open his dad's eyes to the world of modern medicine, but Buck Johnson was stuck on stupid and religion. He never quite understood the balance between religion and medicine. He truly believed that God created certain illnesses for people when he wanted to take them to heaven. Ignorance is bliss and Buck was the poster child for it.

During Eddy's senior year in high school, his younger sister Karen who was just a sophomore in high school thought she was pregnant. She didn't have the courage to tell her parents about her discovery. Karen was smart enough to recognize how ignorant her parents were. Though she did not learn from her older sister Katrina's mistake, she knew that she didn't want to go down the same path as her sister if she was pregnant. Karen wanted to deal with her alleged pregnancy on her own or at least with the support of her brother, Eddy, if need be.

She wrestled with the idea of telling nobody of her possible pregnancy, but after a while she realized that she couldn't go it alone. She told the only person she trusted, which was her older brother, Eddy. He was angry with his sister for allowing herself to get in that situation to begin with, but Eddy eventually came around and was the supportive brother that his sister needed him to be.

Eddy always felt that he contributed to his sister's mishap. Those late night talks they started having about sex, became regular talks. Over time, they both wondered what it'd be like to actually have sex. Curiosity got the best of Karen, and she was persuaded to sleep with Michael, the church's pastor's son. Eddy didn't even know much about sex himself. He was just recycling everything that he had heard from the other boys at his high school. Those guys used to brag about sleeping with women like it was going out of style. It was the same conversation during the bus ride to school every morning, at lunch, during class, and during the ride back home after school. Sex was endless and each story was more intriguing than the last. Although most of it was repetitive, the kids on the bus yearned to hear more of it everyday from different students.

Eddy was always quiet, but he listened and took mental notes of what he heard. This was the closest he ever came to having a conversation about sex. His parents were too hung up on being Christianity to discuss sex with their children. The topic was off limits especially after their oldest daughter, Katrina, became pregnant when she was still in high school. They used Katrina's pregnancy to scare the other two into celibacy. The father did, anyway. How many children really take what their oldest siblings did as a lesson for their own life? The Johnsons did not create an open line of communication with their children.

47

The old saying "do as I say" was supposed to be the motto in the household, but nothing was being said. The kids found out about everything on the streets. Well, Eddy did and he passed it on to his sister.

Eddy knew what the consequences would be if his sister was pregnant and he did not know whether he wanted her to go through the same ordeal that his sister, Katrina, went through when she got pregnant. He simply left the decision up to Karen to make and he wanted to support her in every way. Eddy and Karen had grown very close since Katrina left home. The two of them did almost everything together. They were only a couple years apart and they both hated the way the parents treated them.

Karen was under a tighter leash because she was a girl. Eddy was given a lot more freedom as a boy. She was under more scrutiny, and her parents made sure she was always under their watchful eyes. Karen couldn't even go to the corner store by herself. Her dad was always suspicious and he threatened to kick her out of the house everyday if she ever got pregnant. Even Eddy was tired of his father's threats against his sister. One day Eddy blew his top and told his father to leave his sister alone. He told his father that he was making them pay for the mistake of Katrina, and that was not fair. His father felt disrespected and told them that as long as they were living under his roof, he was going to tell them what to do and how to do it.

Esther Johnson, the wife of Mr. Johnson and mother of Katrina, Karen, and Eddy never even tried to stand up against her husband. She allowed the verbal abuse of her children to continue on a daily basis. As a mother, she would sometimes try to console her kids after their father lashed-out at them, but she would never let her husband know she was doing that. Eddy didn't like the fact that his mother showed weakness in the presence of his dad. He knew that she was probably a stronger person than his dad, but Mr. Johnson had verbally battered the family so badly that everyone feared him.

The Preacher's Son

Michael was the epitome of perfection in everybody's eyes at the church. He could do no wrong. After all, he was a straight "A" student, the captain of his football team, the star player on the basketball team, the youth ministry director, and he volunteered to help the homeless once a week at a local shelter. Everything about Mike's life was too perfect to be true. All the parents at the church were envious of this young man and they used him as the perfect example of a child when they scolded their own children at home. Most parents at the church used the phrase "Why can't you be more like Mike?!" at one point or another while scolding their children. One would think that he was Michael Jordan or something.

Michael took advantage of the parents' good graces, too. He knew that every parent at the church wanted their daughters to end up with him in a marriage and they wanted their sons to be like him. He was the type of guy who prayed on the weaknesses of others. He used everything to his advantage. Mike had developed an image at his church that was comparable to none. His mother and father praised him every chance they got. They had so many positive stories to tell about their son; sometimes they were just too good to be true.

Mike could do no wrong in the eyes of his parents, Mr. and Mrs. Wallace. They were grooming him to take over the church in the future after his dad retires. His parents assumed that he wanted to follow in his father's footstep as a pastor without ever discussing it with him. But Mike also had a dark side. He was getting tired of being a choirboy. He would go out with his friends after school and commit these petty crimes as a form of adrenaline rush. By the time he reached his senior year in high school, he had become an adrenaline junkie and an avid marijuana smoker. He was able to conceal his dirty deeds from everyone, including his parents.

Mike and his friends would go downtown to Filene's Basement after practice and steal as many clothing items as they could. He would go to the store wearing big baggy clothes so he could stuff stolen items underneath them. He had become so daring that sometimes he would make sure that security was in the store following him before attempting to steal something. Mike believed his choirboy image made him invincible and immune to prosecution. He also wanted to prove to his friends that he wasn't as straight as people made him out to be. Mike relished the fact that some of his close friends thought he was a bad boy outside of the church.

To offset that side of him, Mike created a tutoring program at his church to help other students from his neighborhood that had difficulties in school. Mike seemed like he was almost borderline schizophrenic, sometimes. He had developed so many different personalities that it was getting hard for him to keep up with all of them. He was a young man who was trying to please everyone around him.

Michael also had his eyes on the bad girl of the church. The "bad girl" label had been attached to Karen since she was a little girl. He liked Karen because she was not as conventional as the other girls in the church. She defied convention in every way and Michael loved every aspect of her. He gave her the nickname "Fire Starter", because everything hot that started at the church started with Karen. Though he was a couple of years older than Karen, he found her refreshing and very appealing. They used to flirt with each other a lot in church, but that was the extent of their relationship.

Karen

Karen was never a great student in school. Since she was a child, she always had difficulties learning and her parents never sought help for her. Because her brother and sister were bright, the parents dismissed her as the lazy one in the bunch. They didn't believe that their daughter needed help in order to overcome her difficulties in school. Karen was often disruptive in class and her attention span was very short. She could never sit still for more than five minutes. Her teachers had complained to her parents since she started elementary school, but her parents only knew one way to discipline their daughter. Buck would wear out Karen's behind with his belt after each complaint from a teacher and not even a week would go by Karen would be doing the same thing all over again.

In church, it was the same story. Karen disrupted Sunday school, bible class, service, and whatever else she wanted to disrupt. She would chew and pop gum in church even though it was prohibited. She used to make fun of her teachers and had a very smart mouth. Karen never really cared about the complaints that people brought against her to her parents. Mr. and Mrs. Johnson never really had a hold on their daughter. The beatings and other punishment that she used to receive from her father had become a past time to Karen. She had become immune to the pain of her father's leather belt against her skin. The more beatings she received, the higher her threshold for pain reached. She was becoming devilish, and she didn't care what her father did to her.

Punishment was becoming routine for Karen and she sought attention the only way she knew how. Starting trouble was a way of crying out for help, but Mr. and Mrs.

Johnson believed that Pastor Wallace was the answer to Karen's mischievous ways. By the time she reached age twelve, Karen was smoking in the bathroom at her elementary school with the other girls. It had gotten to the point where she was being suspended monthly for one incident after another.

The fact that Karen might have been suffering from Attention Deficit Disorder was never addressed. Her father continued to try to beat her to a straight and narrow path without realizing that he had already lost handle on his daughter. Only a psychologist could diagnose the correct illness, from which Karen was suffering, but in the Johnson household, God was the psychologist and prayer was the proper medication for all illnesses. Karen could've easily sent her father to jail for physical abuse because that big leather belt used to leave marks the size of a malignant tumor around her buttocks. In her effort to act tough, she kept all the abuse to herself and never said anything to the authorities.

At twelve years old, Karen could have easily been mistaken for a grown woman. Her breasts developed to a size C and the rest of her body was moving right along with her breasts. Karen started messing with the boys at her school downstairs in the basement. She would pinch their butts and feel on their chest as a way of flirting with them. When the school held parties for the special holidays, Karen always had to be separated from the boys. Her dance moves were so seductive and over the top, a special monitor was assigned to her at all times. Karen used to have a field day with her monitor too. She especially loved reggae music because she loved to grind on the boys. And every time the monitor would get between her and the boys, she would walk to the other side of the room with all the boys in tow and the monitor had to keep up.

Without any proof, most the boys at the school started to claim that they had either kissed or felt on Karen at her willing. Most of their claims were unfounded, but because of Karen's attitude in school and around the boys, everybody believed the boys' version. Karen was rather frivolous with her attitude around people, and most of the time misunderstood and misread. She hung around with a rough crowd of friends and she was a little feisty herself. Karen was loud and obnoxious at times, but she had also developed good fighting skills and a temper to match. She was fearless and abrasive.

Despite all the negative characteristics that Karen possessed, she was very respectful towards her brother Eddy. It almost seemed like they spoke a different language around each other. Eddy couldn't understand why people were always making his sister out to be such a bad person. He was the only one who knew the kind of abuse she endured at home, and what it brought out in her. Eddy never allowed anyone to bash his sister. He even started to stand up to his dad to defend his sister.

By the time Eddy reached the age of fifteen years old, he was significantly bigger than his father and his father feared his reactions, sometimes. He was quiet with a deadly streak in his eyes. Eddy felt like he and his sister were placed under a microscope after Katrina was kicked out of the house. He felt like his parents were taking out their frustration on him and his sister for their lack of control on Katrina. He and Karen were also growing tired of the physical abuse that they were suffering at the hands of their father.

One day during an argument with his dad, his father slapped Eddy across the face and it knocked the wind right out of him. Karen was so angry she threatened to poison her father for what he had done. She also told him that if she couldn't poison him, she would kill him in his sleep. The rage in Karen's voice was so real, her father didn't eat any food at the house for a month unless it was prepared in front of him by his wife. He also locked his bedroom door every night when he went to sleep for a long period.

Karen started to put her foot down very early on and her father sensed the change in his daughter's attitude. All the beatings that she had taken from him had mounted to pure hatred for her father. Though her mother was against the way her husband treated the children, she never stood up to her husband or said anything that would go against him. She wanted to be part of a unified front, because it seemed to be the right thing to do at the time.

Karen could only relate and talk to her brother, and she didn't want to see her father abuse him. Even though she was younger than Eddy, she acted like she was his protector most of the time. Karen had also missed her sister since she left. Katrina was her play pal when she was a little girl, and without any notice she woke up and found her sister gone because her father wanted to act like an ass. Karen held a lot of resentment against her dad and even more towards her mother for being submissive to an abusive man.

Doing the Dirty Deed

Mr. and Mrs. Johnson admired Michael so much; they asked his father, Pastor Wallace if he could tutor their daughter, Karen. After discussing it with Michael, they agreed that Karen would go to Michael's tutoring program twice a week after school for help. At first, it seemed like the opportunity that Michael and Karen were looking for. They couldn't wait to start the tutoring sessions at the church.

Under the total guidance and supervision of Michael and Michael alone, the after-school tutoring program was in full fledge at the church in the basement on Mondays and Wednesdays. Mr. and Mrs. Wallace trusted that their son was responsible enough to run his own after-school program, and they also enjoyed the fact that they could always tell their friends how responsible he was. It seemed like there was always a reason behind everything that the Wallaces did when it came to their son.

On Karen's first day at the tutoring session, she did very little homework. She spent most of her time complaining about one thing or another to Mike. As a matter of fact, she was starting to work his nerves. She didn't even bother to bring any homework with her; however, she was cautious enough not to be a total disturbance to the other students who were there. With the assistance of two other tutors from the church, Mike was able to help a few of the students conquer their fears of math and science for the first few days. It was kind of hard for Mike to stay completely focused on the students he was helping because Karen wore some of her most revealing shirts and tightest jeans to the program.

In the past, Mr. Johnson tried his best to keep Katrina from wearing pants and jeans, but the church had changed its old ways. A few of the female parishioners had complained to the pastor about the frigid New England winter weather, and he came to his senses and allowed the women to wear pants like the rest of the modern churches in Boston. It really wouldn't have made much of a difference to Karen, because she was going to wear whatever she wanted to wear, anyway. Karen wouldn't be Karen if she just wore regular pants and jeans. She had to wear the tightest clothes that she could find in order to irk her parents as well as all the other adults at her church.

Despite the fact that the parishioners thought Karen dressed in a threatening and provocative way, Mike enjoyed every minute of it. As a sophomore in high school, Karen looked like a grown woman with a body developed enough to send a grown man to jail for statutory rape. After a while, it became clear to everyone at the tutoring program that Karen was not there to be tutored. She came to the program because her father forced her, but more because she wanted to flirt with Mike until he couldn't resist her anymore. Karen was getting a kick out of seeing Mike sweat over her.

Michael had tried his best to maintain that good image in front of the rest of the students. He was respected and liked by most of the students in the program, because he had helped them improved their grades from the time they started coming to his program. Mike was also smart enough to make the student believe that he would never cross the line with any of them. That is any of them, except Karen. She dominated his every thought and there was no better conquest in his mind.

As much as the Wallaces would have liked for Mike to adhere to their "no sex before marriage" rule, he was laughing behind their backs because as handsome as he was, all the girls at his school were throwing ass at him all the time. Mike was sexually active from the time he was fifteen years old, and his parents had no idea. He went over to the girls' houses after school, and lied to his parents about having extended football and basketball practices. He was banging more girls than Ron Jeremy, the porno star. Mike was an all-around pleaser who wanted to please everyone all the time. He somehow managed to become a pro at it.

As much as Karen flirted with Mike, he didn't know how to react to her advances. He didn't know whether or not she was borderline schizophrenic like him or a complete Sybil. He was going nuts out of his mind for months before he worked up the nerves to say something to Karen. The fact that Karen was very outspoken also instilled a lot of fear in Mike. Since she never held her tongue against anyone at the church, he was afraid that she might not hold her tongue if he said the wrong thing to her. It took him a few months, and one day he finally spoke to her after the tutoring program while the two of them were the last people in the basement. He tried as best as he could to be diplomatic. "Why are you such a pain in the ass in my program?" he asked her. She took his comment as a come-on. "I get nervous around young, handsome athletic boys," she answered. "Is that right?" "Yeah, you make me want to tear your clothes off," she playfully told him.

At that point, Mike thought Karen was a trip and there was no way of figuring her out. He laughed at her comment as he walked passed her to go pick up a few pieces of trash that the other students left on the floor. She extended her hand to cop a feel of his ass and said out loud that his ass felt good. It was then that Mike pulled her towards him and started to French kiss her like she never expected. Her first reaction was receptive, but she turned to her old self again and pushed him off of her. Mike thought that she was playing hard to get because she wanted him to chase her. He pushed her up against the wall and held her firm with his hands as he started kissing her neck and slowly made his way down to her bra. She became agitated and angry and screamed for him to let go of her. He backed off and she asked if he was wimp for giving up so easily.

Karen was one challenge that Mike never anticipated. In the past, he never had to force any woman to sleep with him, and he also never had to fight to convince a woman to sleep with him. Mike was totally confused by Karen's game, so he gathered himself and cleaned up the place as she stood there watching. Finally, after he was about to turn the lights off so he could head out, she grabbed his hand and put it down her crotch and asked if he wanted some of that good stuff. Mike picked her ass up, brought her by the stairs, and sat her down and proceeded to make out with her. He slowly unbuttoned her blouse and buried his face in her chest, sucking on her nipples and her neck. Mike wasn't really as skillful as he thought, but Karen had no one to compare him to. She sat there moaning and groaning and touching Mike all over. And finally he pulled off her pants and she unzipped his pants as they continued to make out. The bulge in Michael's pants could not be denied, and Karen stroking it back and forth only confirmed her desire to sleep with him.

While they could not contain themselves, Mike grabbed his penis and pulled Karen's underwear to the side and inserted it inside Karen's wet vagina. She was wincing in pain, as it was her first time ever with a boy. She couldn't really take all that Mike was giving to her, but she couldn't let go of that tough outer shell and image that she had built for herself. She took the pain and acted like she had slept with someone before. As much as Mike was enjoying the whole thing, Karen was not getting any satisfaction from him, because it was painful for her. She never thought that having sex would be so painful and Mike was especially rough with her, because he wanted to prove to her how much of a bad boy he was. They were both trying to make moot points at this time. They humped and grinded on each other until Mike exploded inside Karen and let out a big roar like a lion. Even though Karen had never slept with a boy, she knew that Mike had come because of the clamoring noise he made while he was coming.

Karen asked Mike if he came inside of her and he said, "No." Not satisfied with Mike's answer, Karen asked him again if he came inside her. In his attempt to sound macho he told her "You think that I'm one of those minute men who would come that quickly?" She then asked, "What was all that noise for?" He didn't know what to say to her and told her that it was just his sex noise and that every guy has a sex noise. He then asked her, "How come you don't make any noise?" She told him she wanted to keep quiet, because they were at a church.

They really needed to read the book called "Sex for Dummies." Karen asked once more, "You sure you didn't come inside of me?" Mike continued to lie to her, and told her he did not come. She knew he was lying also because some of his semen started running down her leg as she stood up to pull her pants back up. They were both lying to each other, but she couldn't lie about the fact that she was bleeding. He told her he noticed blood on his penis, and asked if he was too big for her. She told him, "PPuhlize!! I have had bigger ones than that. It's just that my period is probably coming." Mike's ego was crushed a little bit, so he rushed to shut the lights off while Karen tried to wipe herself clean with some napkins. They left the church without saying another word to each other.

A Weird Moment

A couple of weeks had gone by since Karen had her sexual encounter with Mike. Her menstrual cycle was due on the second Monday of every month, and it usually came like clockwork. She was petrified when she didn't get her period that Monday. All kinds of crazy thoughts went through her mind as she started to think back on the encounter with Michael. She knew that he didn't use a condom and the possibility of pregnancy was very relevant. Karen had also stopped going to Mike's tutoring program, because she felt embarrassed by the whole thing. Mike didn't even try to reach out to her to make sure she was all right.

A week had gone by and no period came. Karen was frantic and she felt the need to call Mike to tell him that she was missing her period. It took a lot of courage for her to even pick up the phone to place that call to him. She knew for sure that if she were pregnant, there was only one possibility who the father might be. As bad of an image as Karen had managed to create for herself, in reality, she was not even close to that image. She had not slept with any boys, and most of the things that she was doing to irritate people were harmless. She merely got a kick out of people making a big deal of her shenanigans. Karen's first sexual experience was with Mike.

The phone rang about three times before Mr. Wallace finally picked it up. It was about six o'clock in the evening and the family was having dinner. He was surprised that Karen was even calling his house to speak to his son. Mr. Wallace had always thought of Karen as a little too hot-to-trot. He had especially cautioned his son not to get caught up with women like Karen. However, his disdain for Karen was only expressed privately to some of the members of his congregation behind closed doors. While he was on the phone with her, he took the opportunity to tell her how fine of a woman she had grown to be, and that God had blessed her with a body that every woman in the church would die for. He also told her that she was one of the most attractive young ladies in the church, and he would especially like to see her come to the church a little more often. Mr. Wallace was a big pervert.

After having somewhat of an awkward conversation with Mr. Wallace for about five minutes, Karen asked if his son was around. He told her sure but they were having dinner at the time and she could call back later. Without hesitation, Karen hung up and told him that she'd call Mike later. Mr. Wallace was trying to whisper a few more words to her, but she didn't give him the chance. He walked back to the dinner table to give his son the message that Karen had called. When his wife asked why he took so long to get back, he told her that he was trying to counsel Karen because she needed Jesus in her life. His wife responded, "That's why I love you so. You always find the time to help those in need." Mr. Wallace just shook his head and said, "That's why the good Lord put me on this earth."

A Restless Night

A couple hours had gone by since Karen's initial phone call to Mike. She waited to hear from him, but he never called. She wasn't sure if Mr. Wallace had given Mike the message that she had called, but she didn't want to sit by the phone to wait for him to call her back. She wanted to call Mike again, but her parents were home and she didn't want them to know her business. There was only a couple of phones in the house, one in the kitchen and the other in Mr. and Mrs. Johnson's bedroom, making it easy for them to listen in on Karen's conversation. She didn't want to take that risk.

The fact that her period hadn't shown rendered Karen restless. She didn't know what to do with herself. She thought about the possibility of having a child, but that thought soon went away when she realized that her father would probably kill her for getting pregnant. Karen also started thinking about her other options as well. Since she wasn't too much into Mike, she didn't even think about being married to him. She knew that if she told her parents and his parents that she was pregnant they would force her to marry him, but she knew that she couldn't be tamed at the tender age of sixteen. Karen didn't want to be tied down with a baby and a husband at such a young age.

She soon realized that she might really be faced with the same decision that Katrina had to make when she got pregnant. Karen was tough, but she wasn't tough enough to be on her own. And this was one kind of news that she couldn't take to her parents, because the pastor at her church had been stressing to the kids the dangers of premarital sex. She even thought about having an abortion, but that thought soon went away as well because she would need her parents' consent as a minor. Karen was running out of options. The only thing she could do was pray to God that her period was only late, because of all the stress she had endured after having sex with Mike.

Karen knew that she shouldn't have had unprotected sex with Mike, but she made a stupid decision that put her in a situation that was not at all favorable to her. To make matters worse, even after Katrina was kicked out of the house, Mr. and Mrs. Johnson never even took the time to talk to Karen and Eddy about sex. They figured that the pastor touched upon the subject enough on Sundays to get through to the kids. Never once did they think about a personable parental approach about the subject with their children. Karen really felt that if they had taken the time to talk some sense into her, she might not have slept with Mike.

That night, Karen didn't watch any of her favorite shows on television. She was too busy worrying about her next move if she were pregnant. By eleven o'clock, she had fallen asleep hoping for a miracle to happen the next day when she woke up. It was an unusual night for Karen too, because her brother Eddy religiously went to her room every night to chat with her before they went to sleep. She didn't even have Eddy to listen to her sorrow that night. For some reason, he just did not go to her room that night. She fell asleep clutching her pillow in a fetal position.

Karen tossed and turned that whole night and it was hard for her to get any real sleep. It would be an even longer day the next day when she woke up, because she had to wait until she got out of school to seek Mike to talk to him. When Karen woke up the next morning and noticed that her period still hadn't come, she was losing her mind. She even started to contemplate suicide. She thought about swallowing enough aspirins to put her to sleep indefinitely while she was in the bathroom getting ready for school. At the sound of her brother's knocking on the door to use the bathroom; she woke out of her nightmarish thoughts. Eddy needed to get in the bathroom to get ready for school himself, and he told his sister if she didn't come out he was going to break down the door. Karen and Eddy fought over the bathroom every morning before school.

Karen finally made her way out of the bathroom and said nothing to her brother. Eddy knew that his sister was bothered by something when she didn't say anything to him, so he asked her "what's wrong?" as she walked by him. She told him that nothing was wrong. She went to her room to get dressed and walked down to her bus stop to head to school. That day at school, the teachers noticed a change in Karen's behavior also. She wasn't being her usual disruptive self, but she wasn't participating in class either. Her body was in school but her mind and spirit were somewhere else. She didn't even want to be bothered with the people that she normally hung out with at school. The possibility of being pregnant dominated Karen's thoughts and she wouldn't have peace of mind until she spoke with Mike.

The Confrontation

When school finally let out, Karen made her way to the First Baptist Church in Dorchester to meet with Mike. She was agitated, frustrated, confused and most of all, scared. She needed someone in her corner for support and comfort, and she was hoping that Mike would show his support for what she was about to tell him. As usual, when she entered the tutoring hall in the basement, Mike and the other tutors were helping a group of students with a science project. Karen pulled out her notebook and started writing what she wanted to say to Mike down on a piece of paper. She did not know what kind of reaction to expect from him, but she was hoping for the best. After writing some of her key points down, she became bored and started drawing pictures of a baby on her note pad.

Karen sat through the tutoring program for two hours while Mike helped the other students without saying a word to him. He didn't even bother to greet her, and that set a red flag in her mind. She knew that they hadn't spoken in a couple of weeks, but he was acting like he didn't know her, all of a sudden. She paid him no mind, because she didn't want any of the other students in her business. She had something to discuss with Mike privately.

Meanwhile, Mike looked a little suspicious and was even sweating a little by the presence of Karen in the room. He kept his head down the whole time while he was helping the other students and avoided eye contact with Karen. It was almost like he felt guilty for doing something to Karen that he shouldn't have done. Mike knew damn well that he had ejaculated inside Karen that day when they had sex, and he knew that there was a chance of her becoming pregnant. Not that Karen added to the pressure that he was under, but she would smile every time he tried to sneak a peek at her from the corner of his eyes. She kept her eyes fixated on him after a while, because his curiosity kept forcing him to take a peek at her.

It seemed like Mike was trying to glance at Karen in some sort of weird way in an attempt to try to decipher her body language. He knew he was in for something, but he didn't know what. The last thing he wanted was for Karen to get loud with him in front of the other students. He wanted to make sure that the wild streak in Karen was tamed until tutoring session was over. As much of a fool he thought Karen was, he was even a bigger fool to think that she would divulge her personal business in front of other people. She was able to somewhat manage her personality when she wanted to, and that day she definitely showed her behavioral management skills and self-control.

The moment of truth finally came after the last student threw her backpack over her shoulder and headed out the door. Karen slowly approached Mike and asked him why he didn't return her call. He didn't really know what to say to her, so he came up with an excuse. He told her that he had a lot of homework, and by the time he was done with his homework it was too late to call her house. It seemed well enough and she bought it. She told him that she needed to talk to him and it was better if he sat down. By this time, Mike was sweating bullets and would probably wet his pants at the sound of a mouse. He knew it was going to be the inevitable and he was not ready. Karen sensed his discomfort, so she tried to reach out and grab his hand for security. He pulled his hands away from her and told her to say whatever it was that she had to say.

The meaner side of Karen resurfaced as she told him, "Suit yourself! I'm here to tell you that I might be pregnant and the baby is yours, 'cause I ain't been with nobody else. There, I said it!" Mike's mouth almost hit the floor when the word "pregnant" came out of Karen's lips. The jig was up and Mike had to either claim responsibility or deny that it was his. Unfortunately, he did what most scared teenager and most men would do and said to Karen, "There's no way that you're pregnant by me, because I didn't come inside of you. As much as you have slept around, you better go somewhere else with that shit."

Karen couldn't believe her ears. She jumped across the table and smacked Mike dead in his face as hard as she could. He fell to the floor and told her if she touched him again he would beat the crap out of her. The forceful edge in Mike's voice conveyed to Karen that he was very serious and she had better not trip again. She wanted to try the diplomatic approach and told Mike that she had never slept with anybody other than him, and that if he didn't want to help her perhaps his parents would be happy to hear about their little fling. That was as diplomatic as Karen could get. Mike saw it as nothing but blackmail and was outraged.

Mike went into a futile diatribe saying, "You think a little ho like you can go to my parents and tell them that I slept with you and they would believe you? Everybody in the church already knows your reputation as a ho, and there's no way that people would take your words over mine. You've caused nothing but problems in the church since you were twelve, and now your skank ass want to tell me that you're pregnant with my baby? Bitch, please!"

The forceful edge that he had in his voice earlier had lost its effects after he called Karen a bitch. She jumped on him and started punching him all over his face and body.

He had to run away from her and stand across the table to keep her from getting to him. Karen was pissed that Mike had only thought of her as ho and she didn't want to talk to him about the pregnancy anymore.

She simply told him "God don't like ugly. You're gonna get what's coming to you. It may not be today, it may not be tomorrow, but you're gonna get yours. I shouldn't have never allowed myself to sleep with your sorry ass and if I'm pregnant, I'm gonna keep it just to show your dumb ass parents how perfect their little son is. A blood test will not lie and the only way you can say you're not the father is through a blood test. You just opened a whole new can of worm for your ass, chump!"

Karen walked out the door leaving Mike bewildered without saying another word. He couldn't even fathom what Karen's next move was going to be, but he knew that he had made a big mistake by calling her names. As confident as Mike sounded about his image with the people at the church and his parents he also knew that if subjected to a blood test   that paternity could easily be established, and he could be determined as the father of Karen's baby. Mike was in a catch twenty-two situation.

A Bloody Mess

When Karen left the tutoring program the previous day, she had hoped to never see or speak to Mike again because he was a jerk. She was convinced she was pregnant and she was trying to figure out a way to deal with it. She knew that her brother would support whatever decision she wanted to make, but the fact of the matter was that she still needed her parents to sign for her to have an abortion if she decided to have one. Karen started to get a little depressed that day in class, but when all the students started pointing at her and laughing as she walked down the hall to her next class; Karen wondered what the hell was so funny. She didn't know why people were pointing at her, and she became very confrontational with one girl. She went up to the girl and grabbed her by her hair and asked her if she wanted to get her ass beat for laughing at her. The other student was so scared; she took off running and left behind a big chunk of her hair in Karen's hand.

Karen was going down the hall confronting all the students and they were all too scared to tell her why they were laughing at her. As she got near her class, one of her friends pulled her to the side and told her that her pants were bloody red from the crotch down. Karen ran to the bathroom to take a look and she noticed that there was blood running down her legs. Any other time Karen would have been upset, but that day, she was happy and relieved that an embarrassing situation brought ease to her state of mind. She stood in front of the mirror and smiled a sigh of relief. She bowed her head for a few minutes and gave thanks to God for giving her a second chance. Karen was happy that she was not pregnant and felt like a load had been lifted off her shoulders.

Karen had come to the conclusion that she was pregnant, because her period was almost a week late. She did not even bother to bring a pad or a tampon with her to school. In the past, she was always careful; she either wore a tampon or brought one with her at school when her period was expected. This time she endured the embarrassment at school and was particularly angry with the students who were laughing at her, but she was relieved that she was not pregnant. None of the students knew what Karen was going through in her life because of her tough outer shell which she always used as a defense mechanism. No one got close enough to know her.

Karen was able to go to the nurse's office to get a tampon to keep the blood from running. The embarrassing smell of the blood was something she didn't want to take with her on the bus on the way home. She asked the nurse to use her phone to call her father to pick her up from school. Her father was at work at the time, so she decided to call her mom instead to explain what had happened and her mom was very sympathetic. Her mom called her dad to explain the situation, but it was a different situation when Mr. Johnson got on the phone to speak with his wife. He thought Karen was negligent, and that he shouldn't have to leave work to go pick her up at school just because she had created an embarrassing situation for herself. Mr. Johnson acted like a jerk and told his wife that Karen would have to find her own way home, because he wasn't leaving his job early to go pick her up.

Karen broke down in the nurse's office after her mother told her that her dad wouldn't pick her up. Knowing how distressing the situation was for Karen, the nurse offered to take her home. Karen was grateful, and asked the nurse if she could stay in her office until the end of the school day. The nurse didn't really have much of a choice. She knew that if she had sent Karen back to class it would have resulted in a fight, because everyone at the school was aware of Karen's temper. The nurse tried as much as she could to help Karen clean some of the blood off her pants with alcohol. She also found out that day that Karen was not as bad as she portrayed herself to be at school. They spent a few hours talking, and the nurse learned that Karen was a frightened little girl who didn't want to end up like her older sister. She even told the nurse about her pregnancy scare.

Karen, for the first time, was able to discuss sex and the precautionary measures that she needed to take to avoid getting pregnant if she was to continue to be sexually active. The nurse was really delicate and overly nice with Karen. She highlighted the fact that Karen didn't need to sleep with boys to validate herself to anybody. The nurse explained to Karen that any woman with self esteem would wait for the right man to come along before she decided to have sex, and that her body was her temple and she needed to take care of it. Karen learned a lot about her body, sex, boys, and nurse Baker. In a way, she was glad that her day happened the way it did, because it taught her a lesson and she discovered new things that she wouldn't other otherwise have known.

Peace of Mind at Last

After nurse Baker dropped Karen off at home, she ran directly to Eddy's room to let him know the good news. Everything seemed to work out perfectly that day because Eddy had switched his scheduled day off with another worker at his part-time job to help alleviate his sister's worries. When he left for school that morning, he knew that his sister didn't seem right to him, and he wanted to make sure that he was home to talk to her after school.

Karen didn't even bother to knock on Eddy's door before she entered. He was a little startled when she barged in, but he held his arms open to give her a hug after seeing her standing there. He didn't know what state of mind she was in, but he wanted to console her. Though Karen was happy about not being pregnant, tears of joy started running down her face when she saw her brother standing there waiting to hug her. She knew that he would've been there for her, but the gesture he made towards her confirmed the closeness of the relationship that they already shared. Karen had always felt misunderstood by everyone except her brother, and he had shown that he would be there for her even in her darkest hour.

She tried as much as she could to fight back the tears. They came rolling down her cheeks and Eddy just held her tight against his body as he told her that everything would be all right. Karen nodded her head in agreement, and told Eddy that she knew for sure that everything would be fine because her period had finally come. They both started jumping and dancing around in Eddy's room. Eddie offered to take her down to Brigham's, a neighborhood ice cream parlor in Mattapan Square to celebrate. First, he wanted to talk to his sister about not repeating the same mistakes ever again. Eddy was very frank with his sister about keeping her legs closed and not giving in to the temptation of these young boys on the street. He also told her that they didn't really have a concrete plan if she had indeed become pregnant, and she was just lucky.

After Karen explained how the whole thing initially happened with Mike, Eddy was a little irate because his parents were always quick to throw Mike's name in their faces like he was a saint. Eddy felt like Saint Mike was manipulating everyone at his church, including his parents. He wanted to get back at Mike for treating his sister so disrespectfully, so he came up with a plan to make him sweat for the next few months. Karen was more than eager to make Mike pay for the way he treated her, so she jumped right on board with Eddy's plan.

Sweating It Out

For the next few months Eddy and Karen would have their way with Mike. Eddy had his sister showing up at Mike's school wearing a small pillow under her shirt that made her look like she was carrying a baby. Each time Karen showed up at the school, she antagonized Mike as much as she could with threats of naming him as the father at the hospital, and forcing him to take a blood test to establish paternity. She told Mike that he wasn't going to go away to college to become this big football star that he had planned on becoming, because he was gonna be playing daddy at home. The more she talked, the more it was driving him crazy.

Karen really got to Mike one afternoon when she threatened to take the pregnancy to his parents and the church if he didn't start owning up to his responsibilities. Mike didn't know what to do with her after a while. The more scared of the situation he became, the more she pushed him. Eddy even got in on the fun when he started to call Mike at home to tell him that he hoped he'd be a good brother-in-law and a good father to his nephew or niece. Mike feared that Karen might have told her parents about the pregnancy if she told Eddy. Karen's parents had not gotten in touch with Mike's parents yet; however, he knew he had to keep his cool in order for her not to let the cat out the bag.

One day Karen called Mike and told him that she had a doctor's appointment and asked if he was gonna take her. He told her to get the hell out of his face, that he had his tutoring program to run, and he didn't want anything to do with the baby. As scared as Mike was, he was still trying to stand his ground as a conniving liar. Karen threatened to come to his tutoring program with her stomach showing. He knew that if she came to the program looking pregnant the other students would tell the whole church how pregnant she was, and it would be a matter of time before she revealed he was the father. He agreed to go to the hospital with her. He asked the other tutors to cover for him while he made plans to meet Karen at the hospital the next day.

Meanwhile, Karen wanted to milk her little game for all she could. She found reasons to stop attending church on Sundays with her parents so Mike couldn't see that she wasn't really pregnant. She told Mike that she would meet him at Massachusetts General Hospital at 3:30 pm the next day and to wait for her because she might run a little late. As planned, Mike went to the hospital and waited for two hours for Karen to show and she never did. He went to the front desk to enquire about an appointment for a Karen Johnson, but the nurse told him that no such person existed in her appointment book. Mike was furious and angry that he had gone all the way down to the hospital and Karen didn't show up.

Mike was so pissed when he got home, he didn't even bother calling Karen for an explanation. She, however, called him to tell him how sorry she was for telling him to go to Massachusetts General Hospital to meet her when her appointment was actually at Boston City Hospital. Mike could sense she had a smirk on her face as she told him that, so he hung up the phone in her face and vowed that he'd get her back for humiliating him.

A Game Gone Wrong

Karen and Eddy had exhausted every opportunity to make Mike angry, and Mike had had enough. Mike had conjured up his own plan to get even with Karen. She had called Mike about another appointment at Boston City Hospital, but this time he offered to pick her up from school in his dad's car. Karen thought she was going to play another one of her jokes on Mike, but it turned out that she would be the one getting a dose of a serious medicine.

Mike showed up at Karen's school right when the last bell rang at the end of last period. He had parked his father's car around the corner and walked over to meet Karen at the front. He wore a black baseball cap to hide his face with a black a pair of jeans and sweatshirt. Since Karen knew that he was going to pick her up, she ran to the bathroom to put on the pillow to carry her fake stomach as planned so she could have her little fun with Mike. He still had no idea that she wasn't really pregnant, but he was tired of her game.

Karen got in Mike's car, and told him to head towards Boston City hospital. Her plan was to get him there, and after they got there she would tell him that she mixed up the days for her appointment and he would have to come back the following day to take her back to the hospital again. She thought she had her plans laid out. Mike however, decided to take Karen for a little ride a little farther north than she had intended. He drove up to New Hampshire with her instead, and when he got to a wooded area he told her to get out of his car. Karen fought him and told him she wasn't getting out and he couldn't force her out because she was pregnant. After telling Karen to get out for about ten minutes while she refused, Mike got out and went to the passenger side of the car to pull her out. They struggled at first, but he finally pulled her out and locked the door. He went back to the driver's side and got in the car and drove off.

Mike only wanted to teach Karen a lesson for messing with him. He drove to the other side of the wooded area to watch Karen cry her little heart out, because she thought she was left stranded. After a half hour of watching her being hysterical, he went back over to pick her up and demanded that she apologize for all the headaches she had caused him. She refused to apologize and an argument ensued. Karen attacked Mike and in an effort to try to defend himself against her, he hit her across the temple with the back of his hand and she fell unconscious to the ground. Mike was so stupid he didn't even check for a pulse or find out if she was breathing. He attempted to revive Karen through CPR but his efforts were futile. He didn't even know what CPR was. He was only trying it on her because he had seen it on television. After about fifteen minutes of calling himself "trying to bring Karen back to life," he realized that he might have had a dead corpse in his hands.

Mike panicked and he immediately picked up Karen's body and threw it over his shoulder to put her in the trunk of the car. As he threw Karen over his shoulder, he felt a cushion against his shoulder and when he pulled up her shirt, he realized she wasn't pregnant at all, and that she had been wearing a cushioned pillow to play a game with him all along. He became angrier because she had played him and now he believed it led to her death. He drove to a U-Haul equipment rental center not too far from where they were and bought a big cardboard box. He then proceeded to go back to the wooded area in New Hampshire. He put the box together and placed what he thought was Karen's lifeless body inside the box under a tree.

What may have started out as a prank ended up being a homicide, he thought. Mike never set out to kill Karen that day, but it seemed misfortune was upon him. His bright future was somewhat distant from his mind as he drove down Interstate 95 South towards Boston after leaving Karen's body in a box to rot. All Mike could think about was life behind bars, and the disappointment that his parents would see in him. He knew that it was a matter of time before someone discovered Karen's body, and all the fingers would be pointed his way because Eddy was in on the game that they were playing. He knew Eddy would tell the police to go after him. Mike thought about ways to get rid of Eddy too when he got back home, but that thought quickly faded because he wasn't really a killer.

Startled

Mike was too shaken to drive straight home. He pulled over on the side of the expressway to think about the consequences of what he had done. He started banging his head against the steering wheel as tears welled up in his eyes. He blamed himself for sleeping with Karen in the first place and he blamed his parents for forcing him to live up to an image that he couldn't really live up to. He was really remorseful about what he did, but he was too scared to think about going to the authorities.

As Mike sat in the car on the side of the road pondering his next move, a Massachusetts State Trooper pulled up behind him to see if everything was okay. Mike was startled when the officer knocked on his window to ask if everything was all right with him. The first thing that came to mind when he saw the officer was that Karen's body had already been discovered. The officer noticed the dry streaks of tears on Mike's face, and he asked if he was okay. He told the officer half-heartedly that everything was fine and that he was sad because he had lost his girlfriend. The officer told him that it was nothing to cry about, because there were a lot more women in the world and he was only a young man and that all men have gotten their hearts broken at one time or another.

Mike wasn't really paying attention to all the gibberish sentiment that the officer was dishing out to him. He was just happy that he hadn't been caught. The officer told him that he couldn't stay on the side of the road, and that he needed to head home to deal with his issues. Mike didn't even wait to hear another word from the officer as he put the car in drive and drove straight home. When Mike got home, every little sound of a police siren increased his paranoia. In an attempt to make sure that he was eliminated as a suspect in her disappearance, he placed a phone call to Karen's house. When Eddy picked up the phone, he asked if he could speak to her. Eddy told him that Karen hadn't gotten home yet, and he told Eddy to let her know that he called. He was surprisingly cordial for a guy who had been tormented by Eddy and Karen for the last few months. Eddy wondered what was up with him, but did not say anything.

They hung up the phone and Mike was a little relieved that Eddy wasn't at all suspicious of him. Although Mike felt guilty about "the accidental death of Karen," he wasn't ready to spend the rest of his life in jail. After all, he had been fooling everybody into thinking how great a young man he was for the sake of his parents. Being normal again however, was going to be a challenged that Mike hadn't yet faced.

Saving Karen Johnson

Dinnertime had come and gone and Mr. and Mrs. Johnson had not seen Karen. They wondered why she did not make it home on time for dinner, but she had done that in the past as well. Karen had missed so many dinners with her family in the past, her father simply told her mother and brother to ignore her after a while and start eating. The Johnson family had to learn to adjust to Karen's behavior, and sometimes they felt like they were walking on eggshells with her because of what happened with Katrina. Mr. Johnson didn't really give a damn about the past, though. He wanted things done his way and it didn't matter what the outcome was.

Also, in the past when Karen didn't make it home for dinner, it was because she wanted to piss off her father for something that he might've done to her. It was normal for Mrs. Johnson to ask her husband if he had done anything to Karen before she went off to school earlier in the day. Mr. Johnson told his wife, "as a matter of fact, I spoke with her earlier while I was at work because the school had called me about her disrespecting a teacher. I told her she was gonna get a beating when she got home and that's probably why she ain't here."

Mr. Johnson went on to explain to his wife and Eddy his plan to send Karen to military school in order to save her life. He felt like he was losing control of his daughter, and she no longer feared him or reacted to his threats. As much as Mr. Johnson hated the fact that he had pushed one of his little girls out of his life, he didn't want to lose a second one and he was willing to do whatever necessary to make things right for Karen. Mrs. Johnson had a lot to do with his new way of thinking. She began to slowly to assert herself when it came to the decisions regarding the family by empowering her husband. She would make suggestions to him and fooled him into thinking he was the person that came up with the plan. She took away the threatening feeling that her husband had for many years.

Mr. and Mrs. Johnson were very excited about their new plans for their daughter. Even though Eddy didn't agree with them totally, he knew that his sister needed more structure than his parents could provide. He thought that military school might do her some good. Eddy loved his sister and wanted the best for her as well. Of course, he did not want her to leave him alone in the house with his parents. Although severely misunderstood, he also knew that she wasn't a completely responsible person. If anything, he wanted the military experience to scare her straight, because he knew that she wouldn't stay there for too long. Eddy was the only person who understood that Karen didn't like restraints, and if she felt that people were trying to hold her down she would find a way to get away from them.

It was decided at the dinner table that night, Karen would be transferred to a military school in upstate New York as soon as her parents could make the arrangements. Eddy was told to keep quiet about the plans, and Mr. and Mrs. Johnson were going to ease up on her so she wouldn't suspect anything. It was painstakingly hard, especially for Mrs. Johnson, to discuss sending her child to some military school to straighten her out. She felt like she had failed her daughter as a mother, but she couldn't stand by and allow her to drift away to nothing. She wanted started to want more out of life for herself now, but she also wanted a lot more for her children.

The Agony of a Missing Child

The clock on the kitchen wall read nine o'clock in the evening, and there was still no sign of Karen. Everyone knew that she had never stayed out that late before during a school night, but they hadn't started to worry yet. Karen was always unpredictable to her family, and they were used to her erratic behavior. They were ready to deal with one more of her surprises. Mrs. Johnson didn't want to appear worried, but her facial expression and body language said otherwise. By midnight when her husband shut the television off to go the bed, she asked him if he was going to sleep knowing that her baby girl still hadn't come home.

He responded, "There's nothing I can do at this time. I'll deal with it in the morning because the police department won't take a missing report unless she's been gone for twenty four hours." Mrs. Johnson had to beg her husband to call the police to demand that they do something about her missing daughter.

That day, the Johnson family learned that reporting a missing child is easier said than done, especially a missing black teenager. When Mr. Johnson dialed the police station to ask to speak to someone about his missing daughter, he was immediately asked how long she had been gone. When he told them that she was missing since the end of the school day; they told him exactly what he hadn't expected to hear, that it hadn't been long enough to file a missing report on his daughter.

Furthermore, they started grilling Mr. Johnson about his relationship with his daughter. And the fact that he and Karen had a disagreement earlier in the day also played a big factor in the police stagnancy with the report. Mr.

Johnson was told that he had to wait a full twenty-four hours from the time that his daughter got out of school to report her missing, because it was the last time she was seen by someone. The Police Department also assumed that it could have been an act of defiance from a daughter toward her father.

Meanwhile, Mrs. Johnson spent the whole night tossing and turning in her bed. Eddy also could not sleep, and he did not understand why his sister would want to take a threat from his father this far. Karen never feared a beating from her father and Eddy knew that. He figured it had to have been something a lot more serious for Karen to stay away from home. He kept tossing and turning, trying to figure why his sister hadn't come home. Karen also failed to tell Eddy that she was going to run a prank on Mike on that day. She didn't get a chance to call Eddy to tell him about it, because Mike picked her up from school.

The fact that Karen was missing did not seem to interfere much with Mr. Johnson's sleep. From down the hall, he could be heard snoring in his room. Eddy was worried about his sister, but he worried more about his mother. He knew that she couldn't handle losing another child. After Katrina left, Mrs. Johnson was never the same. She anticipated a knock on the door from her daughter every single day for the first five years, and every knock on the door only intensified her anticipation of Katrina's return. It almost drove her insane, and Eddy didn't want to have to relive that episode all over again. He tried his best to reassure his mother that Karen was fine and that she would eventually come back home.

The whole evening came and went and there was still no sign of Karen. Her parents drove to her school to see if she showed up, but she didn't go there either. Mr. and Mrs. Johnson drove straight to the police station after leaving the school to file a missing report on their daughter. They used the recent picture that Karen took at Sears that Mrs. Johnson kept in her wallet to help the police identify Karen when and if she is found. Mrs. Johnson was sobbing uncontrollably, and she couldn't maintain her composure. The police officer who was taking the report sympathized with her, but it would take a veteran like Officer John O'Malley to help make the process easier on Mrs. Johnson. He understood exactly what she was going through, because during his five years on the force he had encountered many similar cases and the outcomes weren't always positive.

His assignment to the "special missing children unit" propelled Officer O'Malley's desire to become a detective. After completing the missing report, Officer O'Malley advised Mrs. Johnson to put up posters of her daughter around the neighborhood in case someone had seen her.

The Ends Justify the Means

Karen had been missing for over a week and the police hadn't gotten a clue yet. Detective O'Malley asked his superior officer if he could be assigned to the case. It was the first case that was assigned to him in a long time, and it would bring him closer to the family than he ever wished. Detective O'Malley worked relentlessly to find clues and a link to Karen's disappearance. He talked to everyone who knew Karen and from the stories he heard, she didn't have too many friends. Most people could only recall a negative encounter with Karen, which placed O'Malley at a disadvantage. However, the one person that would bring him closer to a suspect was Eddy.

Eddy explained to Officer O'Malley about the little game that he and his sister conjured up against Mike because he had disrespected her after they slept together. As many people Detective O'Malley spoke to about Karen, it was her brother that he found to be the most helpful. He explained to the officer how his sister had lost her virginity to Mike, and he had turned his back on her when she thought she was pregnant. Though Officer O'Malley felt it was a cruel joke that Eddy and Karen played on Mike, he still felt that it didn't warrant her disappearance.

Armed with the information that he received from Eddy, O'Malley went to the Wallace home to speak to Mike. When he arrived at the Wallace home, Mike hadn't gotten home yet. He spoke with Mike's parents and told them that he needed to talk to Mike, because he was known as a friend to Karen. The whole church knew of Karen's disappearance, and the Wallaces were more than cooperative with the police. They assured Officer O'Malley that they would give their son the message and they would also make him available for questioning.

When Mike got home that evening he was shocked to learn that a police officer had come to his house to question him about the disappearance of Karen. The pressure was on, and he didn't know what to do. He felt like he had no one to speak with about his situation, and even worse he felt ashamed for what he had done. The fake image that Mike was trying to uphold had caught up to him and he was not ready to face the music.

Mike sat in his room and started thinking about all the bad things that he had been doing and all the witnesses who could jeopardize his freedom. He thought about the times he and his friends went down to Orchard Park Projects to get high everyday. He thought about the time he went to Filene's and Macy's to steal clothes just for the thrill of it. He thought about the many women he had used and abused to get his way. Mike thought about all the times he had cheated on the field by shooting steroid to get bigger and stronger than his opponents on the football field. He had done so many wrongs, and yet his parents and people at the church thought he was the perfect gentleman. How would he explain all the bad things that he had done when it was all found out? He thought. It was something that Mike didn't have the solution to.

Mike did the only cowardly thing that he could muster the courage to do. He pulled out a pad of paper and a pen, and wrote down his confession before he swallowed a whole bottle of ibuprofen. By the time his parents discovered his body in his bedroom, Mike's heart had given up and there was nothing the paramedics could do to revive him. In Mike's confession however, he didn't leave any clues as to where the police could find Karen's body. He only confessed to what he thought was murder.

A Woman on a Mission

When Mrs. Wallace discovered her son's body in his room, she was hysterical as she ran to her husband to let him know that their only son had taken his life. His body was lying on his bedroom floor with no life left. Mrs. Wallace cradled her son's body until the paramedics arrived. She talked to her son and told him how much she loved him and that he could have come and talk to her before taking his life. Mrs. Wallace was also clutching in her hand, the suicide note that Mike left behind describing the details of the dark side of his life.

Mr. Wallace fought back tears as he stared at his son on the floor. He wanted to be strong for his wife, but he was too angry with her. He started blaming her for forging an image that Mike had to live up to. Mrs. Wallace always wanted to be part of high society, and as a result everyone in her family had to live up to the hype that she created about her upscale family. It was Mrs. Wallace who talked her father into allowing her husband to take over the ministry at the church after his retirement. Mr. Wallace was never interested in becoming a pastor, but his wife pushed him to take on the role and he accepted it as a way to please her. He felt like he was always trying to please his wife and he didn't want to do it any longer. Mr. Wallace missed out on a lot in his son's life, because his wife kept the boy busy doing things in the community for her own benefit.

Mr. Wallace never got to spend time with the boy, since his mother had mapped out his life from the time he was born. The only thing that Mike ever enjoyed doing was playing football with his friends, but his mother didn't see any reason why he should play football with his friends just for the fun of it. She forced him to join the football team in high school, and she pressured him to compete with everyone and everything in his life.

Mrs. Wallace gained her competitive spirit when a man who married her best friend dumped her. The man was a physician, and she became caught up with his profession and his high profile image in the community. He thought she was too stuffy for him, and she wanted to run his life. Her best friend however, was easygoing and attentive and they got along very well. The man decided to pursue a relationship with her best friend and they married a year later and had a son. Mrs. Wallace married her husband who was an accountant and a member of her church a year later as well. She tried to talk her husband into getting his MBA, and when he refused she forced him to become a preacher because it would bring prestige and adulation to her family. Mrs. Wallace wanted to be with a prominent man to show her ex that she was worthy.

Mrs. Wallace also gave birth to Mike who was about the same age as her ex-best friend's son. Her friend's son was a natural born athlete and leader who always made the high school sports headlines in Boston. In order to continue her competition with her ex-best friend, Mrs. Wallace forced her son to become an athlete and a leader. Mike never understood the motivation behind his mother' aggressive push for him to be great at everything, but her husband knew very well where her intention came from. Her break-up with her ex was the talk of the church for a long time, and Mr. Wallace ended up paying the price because his wife was a woman scorned.

Concealing the truth

Mr. Wallace finally asked his wife if Mike revealed any reason why he took his life in that letter. At first, she ignored his question because she knew what he was saying sounded too familiar. Mike had written on the note that he was tired of living up to an image that his parents had created. Now that he was gone, Mrs. Wallace didn't even want to face the reality of the situation. Her husband asked to see the letter, and she refused to give it to him. He demanded to see his son's last words, and before she handed it to him she asked him to promise that he wouldn't go to the police with it. Mr. Wallace didn't understand why he would have to conceal a suicide note from the police, and he told his wife that he would make no such promise.

Mrs. Wallace was up to her old tricks again. Even as a grieving mother, she still wanted to uphold her image. She didn't want people to find out that her son had committed murder before he took his life. The little perfect image she had helped to create was going to stay intact as far as she was concerned. Mr. Wallace didn't want to be part of any conspiracy to hide evidence from the police. He snatched the letter from his wife, and as he read it tears ran down his face. He shook his head in disgust at his wife. She had pushed the kid to the brink of disaster, he thought. He felt bad for never standing up against his wife and for not being a voice for his son.

From the letter, the phrase "You guys have forced me to live up to an image that I couldn't uphold" kept echoing in Mr. Wallace's head. He knew exactly what Mike meant by this. Mike was never given the opportunity to be a normal teenager, and as a result he had led a double life and he kept secrets from his parents. Mr. Wallace was sickened by the whole situation. He told his wife that if she wanted him to continue to be a part of her life, she would have to stop acting so selfishly and stop living for other people. Mr. Wallace lost his only son, and he accepted part of the responsibility for his son's death. The worst part of the letter was when Mike admitted to delivering the fatal blow to Karen's temple. Mr. Wallace knew that his son was no murderer, and it had to have been an accident that he killed Karen.

Mr. Wallace wanted to do the honorable thing by calling the police, and tell them about the letter. The whole congregation had been made aware of Karen disappearance, and they were praying for the best. Mr. and Mrs. Wallace would have to tell them that Karen was killed at the hand of their son, and that was something that Mrs. Wallace was totally against. It would all lead back to her selfish nature. This time however, Mr. Wallace took his position as a man in this relationship and his position as a man of God and called the police to report the suicide and the letter found.

There was rage inside Mrs. Wallace as her husband picked up the phone to call the authorities. Before he could finish his first sentence on the phone, she attacked him and told him that he didn't care about the reputation of his family. She kept swinging at him while he was on the phone, and he kept dodging as he told the cops to get to his house quickly. He finally hung up the phone, and she picked it up and threw it at him in full attack mode. Mrs. Wallace was like a woman possessed, and her husband had no idea that he had made a deal with the devil. He tried to subdue her, but she kept kicking and screaming that she was going to destroy him and that without her he would be nothing.

Mrs. Wallace was saying things to her husband that were unforgivable, and she didn't seem to care. Mr. Wallace, meanwhile, had made up his mind that he was going to leave his wife and the ministry because his wife had crossed the line. He knew that she was on the Board of Directors at the church, and he did not want to have to plead for his job and wanted to wash his hands off with "the crazy psycho wife of his." Mr. Wallace was very tactful in the way that he had planned to leave his wife. He didn't want to end his marriage in turmoil and he wanted to be there for his wife through her bereavement period.

The Moment of Truth

The moment of truth had finally arrived for Mr. and Mrs. Johnson. They were about to receive the worse possible news that any parent could have received about their missing child. It was also one of the worse predicaments that Officer O'Malley had been in since he became a police officer. He had to deliver the bad news about Karen, but even worse he had to tell them that their pastor's son was responsible for her disappearance and he had committed suicide without leaving any clues about the body. Officer O'Malley wrestled with his approach as he had never done this in the past. There was no gentle way to deliver the message to a parent that their child had been murdered. O'Malley had developed a close relationship with Mrs. Johnson through the course of his investigation, and he knew that she had anticipated finding her daughter alive.

The fact that Mrs. Johnson had divulge to Officer O'Malley that her oldest daughter, Katrina had left home pregnant when she was fourteen years old weighed heavily on her heart. He didn't know how much more her heart could take, but he had a job to do. Every conversation Mrs. Johnson started with Officer O'Malley began with Katrina's name, and she had hoped that he would find out information about her whereabouts as well. O'Malley never discovered any information on Katrina, because she had been using the alias Star Bright whenever she was arrested. Easing the pain for Mrs. Wallace was a chore in itself, and O'Malley was just the right person to do that. Though he wasn't always philosophical, O'Malley found a way to make delivering the news to Mrs. Johnson easier.

He knocked on Mrs. Johnson's door early that afternoon, and found her sitting in front of her television watching the news. She was wishing and hoping to find out any little information about her daughter from the mid-day news. But nothing was reported about Karen. It seemed like the media had no interest in the disappearance of a little black girl. There were more important issues to cover like which neighbors' cat had to be rescued from a tree by the fire department or which animals had to be saved from an unkempt shelter. There always seemed to be something more important in the news than the lives of black people.

The only kind of news that the media yearned for was the "shoot 'em up bang bang" that took place among the black people. A good black-on-black, shoot out, murder-rampage would make the headlines any day. The depiction of savages in the hood killing themselves is what the media hungered for. Why would the life of a missing little black girl make the local news? It was common for the local news to report little white girls being kidnapped in states as far as Montana, however. Their lives are more important and national alerts needed to be issued for these white kids.

America's media is so biased that it can be sickening at times, Mrs. Johnson thought.
The police department wanted to inform the Johnson family that someone had confessed to killing their daughter before they went to the media using O'Malley as the messenger. O'Malley tried his best to ease the situation for Mrs. Johnson by holding her hands and showing a lot of sympathy. He told her that someone had confessed to killing Karen, but he had not mentioned where he left the body. Mrs. Johnson almost fell to the floor after he delivered the words. They seemed to cut

through her heart like a knife. What O'Malley feared most was her reaction when she found out that it was Mike Wallace who had confessed to the murder.

When Officer O'Malley finally told Mrs. Johnson that it was Mike who had confessed to the murder, she seemed aloof at first. She then acted in anger and told Officer O'Malley with as many expletives as she could that she never trusted the bastard. Mrs. Johnson was totally devastated, but she knew that her daughter was a fighter and a part of her refused to believe that she was actually dead. She wanted to find the body in order for her to believe that her daughter was really gone. She was angry that Mike had given closure to his parents, but left her bewildered.

Mrs. Johnson never really bought into that perfect image of Mike that everyone had spoken of at the church. She had seen him smoking weed with a group of boys once while coming home from the supermarket. She never said anything because her husband had always tried to use Mike's good image to motivate his own kids, and she didn't know how to tell him that Mike wasn't at all what he appeared to be. Mrs. Johnson also felt guilty, because if she had said something to somebody about Mike maybe her daughter would still be alive.

The Media Nightmare

After the Johnson family was notified of the possible death of their daughter, the police department released a statement to the media about Mike's confession. Immediately the media felt it was a situation that was newsworthy, because a young man whom people believed to have been on the straight and narrow path had committed a heinous crime. Every television station in Boston focused on Mike's suicide and confession. They referred to him as a coward who didn't want to face his fate in the justice system. They had totally forgotten about the young girl who lost her life. When they finally talked about her, they tried as much as they could to find information about her young troubled past.

The Johnson and Wallace families were furious at the portrayal of these two young people in their moments of sorrow. The media even alluded to their love affair as the reason why Mike was pushed over the edge. Everyone was trying to draw their own conclusions. The media succeeded once again in creating the image of the young man as a cruel, calculated murderer while Karen was portrayed as a young female victim who was too hot-to-trot. The media's distorted version of what actually happened had everyone at the church turning their heads at Pastor Wallace and his wife.

Mr. Wallace had decided to tell his congregation that he was stepping down as pastor because he and his wife were getting a divorce the Sunday after his son's burial. The media camped outside the Wallaces' home waiting for a statement, and when that didn't work they went to the church and waited for them there. A few people at the church took the opportunity to let the world know that Mike and Karen were great kids, but those statements never made it to the television screen on the news. Mike's ex-cohorts managed to capitalize on his misfortune by accepting money to talk about some of the bad things that they did together when he was alive. The media had managed to turn Mike's so-called friends against him with a fist full of dollars.

Pastor Wallace's departure from the church was something that he wanted to deal with privately within the church, however, the media got news of his resignation and they drew their own conclusion about that as well. It was not favorable toward Pastor Wallace at all to say the very least. The church didn't really know what to make of everything that came to light that week. It seemed as if the pastor didn't even have a hold on his own family while preaching the good word of the Lord to his congregation.

Mrs. Wallace, meanwhile, fell into a deep depression because everything that she had worked so hard to build was destroyed publicly, and she couldn't face the embarrassment. Mr. Wallace tried his best to be supportive and sought help to get her out of her depression, but she continued to verbally abuse him until he could take it no longer. He walked out on her while she was at the hospital, and left her parents to deal with their lunatic daughter.

Dealing with a New Tragedy

After Mike's confession was discovered and made public, the Johnson Family no longer wanted anything to do with the church. They had discovered that they were around a bunch of fair-weather Christians who ran to the media like parrots with their opinions about the tragedy. Mrs. Johnson didn't want to be around the people at the church anymore because of their judgmental attitudes. When Katrina left a few years earlier they started spreading rumors about her being a little tramp that had to be sent to upstate New York to be tamed. Since it was just a rumor, the Johnsons didn't really know who started it, and they didn't really want to deal with it because she had truly left the house because of her pregnancy.

This time around, things weren't going to be as easy for Mrs. Johnson. With Katrina, she was still hoping that one day that she would walk back into her life, because she had no confirmed report that Katrina was dead. She prayed everyday that Katrina would have a change of heart and would want to reconnect with her family. Mrs. Johnson was very hopeful. She wanted to have the same positive attitude with Karen even though Mike had confessed to killing her. It had to be a mother's hunch.

A few years passed and Karen's body was never discovered. Everyone in the house had grown depressed over her disappearance. Mrs. Johnson stopped all physical relations with her husband and Eddy became a recluse. The Johnson household was not the same without Karen, and everything changed for the worse. Eddy isolated himself in the basement of his parents' house. After he graduated from high school, instead of going to Northeastern University as planned, he took a job as a

Janitor with the Fleet Center and invested all his earned money in turning his parents' basement to an apartment.

Eddy didn't interact much with his father, because he felt that he had contributed to the destruction of the family. His mother also blamed herself for not standing up for her kids when her husband was beating them. A part of her truly abhorred her husband, but as a Christian woman, she couldn't harbor ill feelings towards him. She continued with her wifely duty in the household except when it came to sexual relations. She made sure that Eddy had a plate of food to eat everyday, but it was easy to see that they were a dysfunctional family.

Mr. & Mrs. Johnson

Since kicking Katrina out of the house, Mr. Johnson was trying his hardest to keep Karen under lock and key. Mr. Johnson didn't want Karen, the only daughter he had left, to end up pregnant at a young age like Katrina. The only place he allowed Karen to go to alone was the tutoring program at the church. The fact that he had turned his back on Katrina really bothered his conscience, but he didn't want to show this to his family. His wife, Mrs. Johnson, became very resentful toward her husband... Her eldest child had been gone for a long time and she wondered everyday what became of her. The family never really expected for Katrina to be gone from their lives forever. The stubborn Mr. Johnson allowed his pride to get in the way of finding his daughter.

Mrs. Johnson used to cry herself to sleep at night thinking about Katrina and how she just disappeared from her life. She was so dependent on her husband that she never even learned how to drive a car. From the time she married her husband, Mr. Johnson informed her that he was the man of the house and whatever decisions he made regarding the family, she was to support him. She was a wonderfully subservient wife for most of their marriage; that is, until Katrina was kicked out of the house. Mrs. Johnson missed her daughter so much that she started talking back to her husband. She no longer wanted to listen to his idiotic rants about how a family should be.

Mr. Johnson's idea of a functional family was so out of line with the times that he could easily be mistaken as a man from the Stone Age. He didn't want to accept the fact that his daughter, Katrina, was a good person and that he drove her away. He was constantly suspicious of Katrina for no reason. Katrina had never failed any classes in school and didn't really do many bad things at home for him to think that she was a bad child. Because his wife sat back and said nothing about his parenting, Mr. Johnson thought everything he was doing was correct. He drove Katrina out of the house. This same behavior was now causing his daughter, Karen, to do bad things.

Mr. and Mrs. Johnson never discussed Katrina's disappearance from their lives. Their silence about the whole situation was eating away at Mrs. Johnson's heart. Her husband would be driving her in the car, and she would suddenly see someone and think it was her daughter. One day Mrs. Johnson chased a woman down just because she walked a little bit like Katrina. She saw the lady from behind and was overcome with joy. Mrs. Johnson ran after the lady hoping to give her a big hug. Upon reaching the woman and tapping her on her shoulder, however, she realized it wasn't Katrina because the woman turned around and appeared significantly older. Mrs. Johnson was once again disappointed and had started to become a little delusional even from these random Katrina sightings. She wanted to see her daughter at any and all cost.

While her husband was away at work, Mrs. Johnson would search the phone directory looking for Katrina's name. One day she got on the phone and called about two hundred people whose first name started with the first initial K and the last name Johnson. As a mother, she knew that she had not done right by her daughter. Mr. Johnson had never revealed to the church that he had kicked his daughter out of his home and family because she was pregnant. Instead, he told the congregation that Katrina was sent to upstate New York to live with his mother. He felt that Katrina had brought shame to his family by getting pregnant and he didn't want the church to find out.

As much as it would have seemed like the First Baptist church was a receptive place that would accept everyone with open arms and without prejudice, it was also a place where people gossiped about each other. The congregation could and would have the private business of a family spread from Boston to Tallahassee in a matter of minutes. Rumors and gossip played a big role in the church. The women who held each other's hands and prayed together every Sunday were the same women who dogged each other's families behind their backs. It was understood by the Johnson Family that the church was not always as welcoming as they would have people believe. So, Mr. and Mrs. Johnson made sure that they got their story straight with their children, Karen and Eddy, as far as what they needed to tell the church about Katrina.

The pastor at the church found it odd that Katrina suddenly stopped coming to church with her family. When he asked her father where she was, Mr. Johnson had to lie to maintain his good standing and reputation within the church. The commandment "Thou shall not lie" had been totally ignored by the Johnson Family. In fact, Mr. Johnson was the biggest hypocrite in the church. He had kicked his daughter out of his family's life for lying, and he turned around and asked them to lie to the church about Katrina's absence.

Mrs. Johnson may have been passive and subservient, but she was not naive. She was the one who pointed out to Mr. Johnson how much of a hypocrite he was. She was getting tired of living for people whose opinions had absolutely no significance to her. Mrs. Johnson told her husband that he had allowed his faith in ignorance to destroy their family and she was tired of it. She also reminded him that she was the one who introduced him to the life of Christ, and now he wanted to show her how much more of a Christian he was than her. Mrs. Johnson was furious when she realized that she had lost her daughter for good. The agony and the pain that she suffered over the years was all because her husband did not want to let go of his stubbornness.

As bright and honest as Mr. Johnson wanted to appear to his family, they had lost all respect for him because of his ignorance. His remaining children stopped talking to him after a while, and his wife vacated their bedroom altogether. Mrs. Johnson moved into Katrina's bedroom years after she was kicked out. She had forbidden her other children, Eddy and Karen to ever go into Katrina's room in hopes that her daughter would one day come back home to the family. For years, she went in that room every Saturday and cleaned it spotlessly. She never changed anything in the room, as she needed every little reminder when she thought about Katrina.

Moving into Katrina's room after fifteen years of marriage was the final step to Mrs. Johnson's declaration of independence in the household. She had grown tired of listening to her husband, her pastor, and the congregation at her church with regard to the way she was supposed to live her life. It was because of them that she never set out to find her daughter to begin with. Mrs. Johnson had become bitter towards her husband and her church, but by the time she had decided to do something about it, it was a little too late. Katrina was long gone and she had missed out on the opportunity to see her daughter and grandchildren grow up. Mrs. Johnson prayed and wished everyday that her daughter was okay out there in the world.

Despite all the animosity Mrs. Johnson felt towards her husband and her church, she continued to prepare her husband's favorite meals at home and attend the church with her family every Sunday. Though she and her husband hardly spoke any words to each other, they had created a new way of communicating silently. They were both two miserable souls who were unable to connect to the modern world. Mrs. Johnson couldn't see herself leaving her husband, her children, or her home. The fact that Mrs. Johnson was financially dependent on her husband also weighed heavily on her mind.

In her late forties, Mrs. Johnson was encouraged by Karen and Eddy to do more with her life. First, she had to find a way to earn her GED. With the help of an adult education program and a little extra tutoring, Mrs. Johnson earned her GED by the time her son entered high school. She wanted to be a role model for her children, and she also wanted to show them that it was never too late to accomplish certain goals in life. Mr. Johnson, however, felt threatened by the fact that his wife was able to earn a GED. He had always made it seem like he was the most intelligent person in his household even with a sixth grade education. It was his way of elevating himself while downgrading his wife. Mrs. Johnson started to learn more and more through her readings and writings. She discovered how a lack of education kept her husband in total darkness.

She began to realize why her husband had been acting so ignorantly during the course of their marriage. She wanted to teach him about her discovery and love for reading, but he fought her every time. He even tried to belittle her achievements on a few occasions by telling her that she would never be more than a wife and a homemaker to him no matter how much she had learned through her readings. Though Mr. Johnson quit school in the sixth grade, his reading skills were at a third grade level and he had never tried to improve them. When he went to church with his wife, he pretended he was reading from the bible, but he had actually memorized the scriptures after his wife had read them aloud to him at home. Mr. Johnson had proven that most illiterate people are usually pretty smart at concealing their deficiencies to the rest of the world.

Mr. Johnson concealed much of his life and he wasn't open to any new changes, unless directed by his pastor. In the process, he created a barrier of communication between himself and his wife. It was so important for Mr. Johnson to be the head of his household; he chose to stay ignorant so that he could lead by force instead of common sense and intelligence. It was no fault of his own that Mr. Johnson never finished school, but he was too proud to allow people to know that he was deficient in any way.

Mrs. Johnson decided that she wanted to become a counselor to help other families with various social adjustments and issues and also to be an inspiration to her children. At the urging of her daughter and son, Mrs. Johnson enrolled at UMASS in Boston as a non-traditional student to major in Social Work. In just three years, she completed a Bachelor's Degree, and after graduation she accepted a position at a local center to help families on welfare.

A Forgiven Heart

Eddy felt he had lost both of his sisters because of his parents and their overly religious nature, he did not want to ever set foot in another church again. One night he was having one of his regular talks with Jimmy after a practice session, he mentioned that he had never gotten a chance to grow up with his sisters because his parents had pushed them out of his life. Jimmy could see the hurt in Eddy's face as he expressed this pain. Before he could say anything more about his parents' religion Jimmy asked him "When was the last time that you've been to church?" Eddy was embarrassed to tell Jimmy that he had not been to church for over fifteen years since the disappearance of his sister Karen. Although Jimmy didn't hear the whole ordeal about Karen and Katrina's disappearance from Eddy, he knew that he sympathized with him, because Jimmy himself had questioned his own faith in the past when his mother disappeared out of his life.

Jimmy invited Eddy to his church where the vibrant Pastor Jacobs was able to touch somebody's soul every Sunday. He knew if Eddy came to his church he would see the difference, and he would not hold everyone to the standard of his old pastor. Eddy was apprehensive about the invitation at first. However, after much convincing and a promise from Jimmy that he would never ask Eddy to come back if he didn't like it, Eddy accepted Jimmy's invitation.

Jimmy had talked to Pastor Jacobs the Wednesday before Sunday's service about his good friend, Eddy, and how Eddy was depressed about the loss of his sisters. Jimmy also recalled his own feelings when he learned of his mother's death and how he was able to deal with it through the help of Pastor Jacobs and his sister. The good pastor assured Jimmy that he would have a special service on Sunday about loss and the loss of a family member, sibling, or a close friend. Pastor Jacobs referred to his good book, the almighty Bible, to prepare himself for service on Sunday.

As expected, Eddy showed up at church for the 9:00 am service. Jimmy was very happy to meet and greet him at the door. Jimmy introduced Eddy to his wife, Lisa, his sister, Nina, and Nina's husband and their two children. They all welcomed Eddy like he was family. That Sunday Pastor Jacobs was able to hit a note with Eddy when he talked about letting go and forgiving the sins of others in order to liberate the mind from bondage. Eddy paid close attention to Pastor Jacobs' words and when Pastor Jacobs explained that people sometimes placed too much of their responsibilities in God's hands and religion, he understood exactly where the pastor was coming from. Pastor Jacobs explained that in order for God to help a person, that person must also help himself or herself. As a preacher he is only human and no one should look to him to help solve all of their problems.

Eddy started recalling how his parents relied on prayer for years to solve every little problem without taking the appropriate actions. He also thought about Pastor Wallace, who enforced those beliefs for years, and now he was finding out something different from another pastor who had admitted that he had a dark past himself. Pastor Jacobs had always proudly taken the opportunity to tell the church about his dark past, and how without his past he would not have been a pastor. The perfect image that Pastor Wallace had tried to build was something that Eddy had always had a problem with. He was happy to hear a pastor admitting to human mistakes, and he embraced the words and the wisdom of Pastor Jacobs.

Eddy had a newfound faith in the church. He knew that he had to let go of all the hatred that he harbored over the years toward his father because his dad didn't know better.

Toward the end of service, Pastor Jacobs asked everyone who needed prayer to come to the front of the church, and Eddy was one of the first one to get out of his seat to walk toward the podium. Jimmy also got up to hold his hand for support. Pastor Jacobs asked the Lord to cleanse the souls of the people who harbored ill feelings toward others, and to show them the way to forgiveness. Through the pastor's prayer, Eddy could feel his words going through his spirit. By the end of service, Eddy felt rejuvenated like he had been to a place where the Lord had heard his cries and took away all of his pain.

After church, Jimmy introduced Eddy to Pastor Jacobs and he invited him to have brunch with his family. Eddy was gracious in accepting the invitation to brunch. Everyone drove to The Cheesecake Factory, which was one of Jimmy and Nina's favorite spot for brunch on Sundays. Pastor Jacobs couldn't make it, because he had another service at 11:00 am that Sunday but he promised to continue to pray for Eddy.

Discovering an Illness

As Jimmy and Eddy's friendship grew stronger, they started spending more and more time with each other. Eddy still kept his family life discussion to a minimum because he was still trying to deal with the pain of losing his two sisters. Pastor Jacobs' Sunday service had helped, but it didn't erase Eddy's pain completely. Eddy still needed time to heal. He talked as much as he could with Jimmy about the Bible, and his effort to forgive his mother and father. He also told Jimmy about how he wanted his mother and father back together for happier times. Jimmy encouraged his efforts, and even offered to come by his house to see if his parents would give Pastor Jacobs' church a try.

Everything seemed to be normal in Jimmy's life, and he was very happy that he was able to help Eddy. Even Lisa had taken a liking to Eddy, and she invited him over her house for dinner with Jimmy on many occasions. When Jimmy started feeling restless, had difficulty sleeping, and was tired all the time during the off-season, Eddy was the first person that he told. It seemed as if all of Jimmy's energy was gone, and he didn't know what was going on with him. Jimmy didn't want to tell his wife and sister, because he didn't want them to worry. It was at the urging of Eddy that Jimmy finally went to the doctor to see what was wrong with him.

Unfortunately, Jimmy received the worse news that he could've gotten from his doctor at the Beth Israel Deaconess Medical Center that day. Jimmy was told that there was a possibility that he was suffering from kidney failure during a routine check-up. Jimmy explained to the doctor that he was fatigued all the time, his skin was dry and itchy, he was nauseated and vomiting, there was an abundance of fluid retention, he couldn't fall asleep, his thoughts were confusing, and he had a metallic taste in his mouth all the time. Dr. Morris ordered him to undergo a complete physical the following day. It was then that the doctor discovered that Jimmy's kidneys were failing him. He told Jimmy about the few options that he had as a patient, and one of the recommended options was dialysis. Dr. Morris told Jimmy that he could undergo Hemodialysis treatment for a few weeks. If there was no progress made he would need a transplant if he wanted to continue to live, much less play basketball.

Jimmy was not left with too many choices. After receiving the news, Jimmy called Pastor Jacobs, his sister, and his wife in a meeting to inform them about his health. Everyone was more than willing to sacrifice a kidney for Jimmy. Everyone believed the person with the strongest possible match was Pastor Jacobs because he was Jimmy's father. Without hesitation, Pastor Jacobs scheduled an appointment with Jimmy's doctor to see if he was a possible match. Meanwhile, the Hemodialysis treatment was not working for Jimmy.

When Pastor Jacobs went to the hospital, Dr. Morris explained the pros and cons of a living donor to him, but no negative impact could persuade Pastor Jacobs to think twice about saving his only son's life. Pastor Jacobs was also informed that he could lead a normal active life after recovering from surgery without any special restrictions. "The body can function perfectly with one kidney as long as the donor has two healthy kidneys before the operation," Dr. Morris explained. Dr. Morris also told Jimmy the advantages of a living donor. "A patient who receives a live donor transplant has a better immediate outcome and long-term kidney transplant survival than a patient who receives a deceased donor transplant," he said.

Things looked very optimistic. As required by the hospital, the resident Nephrologist subjected Pastor Jacobs to undergo a thorough evaluation to determine his general health and kidney condition. Pastor Jacobs went through a complete medical history and physical examination. He was tested for diabetes, cancer, high blood pressure, kidney stones, and poor kidney function. An X-ray was taken to evaluate his lungs, an EKG was taken for the heart, a blood and urine test (including HIV testing) was given, a spiral Computed Tomography (CT) scan was administered to determine any abnormalities in the kidneys or the blood vessels that lead to them, and a final cross match to check for antibodies within one week of transplant were all completed. Pastor Jacobs also met with the nurse and social worker at the hospital for an evaluation.

Though the hospital Nephrologist administered many tests, it was determined that Pastor Jacobs was not a match for Jimmy. The process of elimination had begun. Lisa was the next person to see the doctor in an attempt to save her husband's life, but she was not a match either. Nina went through the same process, and unfortunately she also was not a match. Jimmy was starting to get scared, but Nina's husband Collin instilled hope in Jimmy when he offered to go see the doctor to check if he was a possible match. The other people who had offered to donate a kidney to Jimmy were almost automatic, because they were his father, wife, and his sister. Collin didn't have to offer to do it, and Jimmy thought it was very big of Collin to offer him a kidney. Even though he had long considered Collin a brother, it was a gesture that he didn't expect.

Unfortunately, Collin would not be a match either. Meanwhile, Jimmy continued to deal with his illness. He had not been spending time with Eddy. He didn't even tell Eddy about his diagnosis. It was when Jimmy and the Celtics decided to hold a press conference to tell the public about Jimmy's illness that Eddy found out about it. At first, Eddy didn't understand why Jimmy didn't call to tell him about it, but he understood that Jimmy was going through a lot and he had to deal with his family first. Eddy wanted to give Jimmy time to deal with his situation before calling him. He also knew it was unlike Jimmy to go a couple of weeks without calling him.

One More Offer

Eddy finally received a call from Jimmy after a few weeks of dealing with his search for a kidney. When Eddy picked up the phone he could tell that Jimmy wasn't his normal upbeat self and he knew why. Jimmy started explaining to Eddy how things were not looking so optimistic for him, because he had a rare blood type and everyone who had offered to give him a kidney thus far was not a match. Eddy was not overly educated about kidney failure, so he started asking Jimmy all kinds of questions. It almost seemed as if he was prying, but because he and Jimmy had developed such a comfortable relationship Jimmy didn't mind sharing the information with him.

After learning from Jimmy that he could live a long, healthy life with one kidney, Eddy did the most selfless thing he could think of. He offered to give Jimmy one of his kidneys. Jimmy was taken back by Eddy's gesture, but he was not surprised. Jimmy always knew that Eddy had a kind heart, and he didn't want to force Eddy into doing anything out of pity. Jimmy explained to Eddy if death was to be his fate because he couldn't find a kidney, he was alright with that. He didn't want to force anyone to make any sacrifices for him. Jimmy truly believed that he had been blessed during his short life and if the Lord wanted to take him away he was willing to go.

Eddy took a long deep breath on the phone, and he started to address Jimmy in a very emotional tone, "You are the first person in a long time that has taken the time to talk to me and tried to get to know me since I've been working at the Fleet Center. You've never made me feel out of place or less than you. I feel connected to you somehow. If that connection was going to come through by sharing my kidneys with you, then so be it. Donating my kidney to you is not at all a sacrifice, but a situation that God had created to bring together two souls from two different spectrum of the world. The only thing that I would need from you is for you to pay my hospital bill."

Just when Jimmy thought his luck had run out, and there was no way out because the transplant waiting list for a kidney was so long, God sent an angel his way named Eddy. The optimism in Jimmy resurfaced as he asked Eddy jokingly if he could at least take him out to eat so he could have a full stomach when they visited the doctor the next day. Eddy laughed at Jimmy's comment as they made plans to meet for dinner later.

A Meeting by Chance

The next day Jimmy drove himself to Eddy's house in Hyde Park to pick him up for the doctor's appointment. When Eddy rang the doorbell, Mr. Johnson answered the door and he immediately recognized Jimmy as a Boston Celtics player. In fact, Jimmy was his favorite player on the team. Mr. Johnson was a little puzzled, at first, because he didn't know why a basketball superstar would show up at his door. Jimmy quickly explained to him that he and Eddy were friends and he was there to pick him up. Mr. Johnson called for Eddy to come upstairs as Jimmy waited in the living room.

Mr. Johnson and his wife were admiring Jimmy, because they had never seen a basketball star up close and personal before. If Jimmy had examined Mr. And Mrs. Johnson's faces closely, he would have recognized the obvious resemblance, but he was timid and did not want to be treated like a star. He kept his eyes glued to the family portrait hanging on the wall in the living room. In the portrait was a picture of Katrina, Karen, Eddy, and Mr. And Mrs. Johnson. While staring at the picture, it was as if Jimmy almost recognized his mother even when she was a little ten year-old girl. He chose not to say anything to Mr. and Mrs. Johnson because Jimmy was not the type to believe in coincidences. As far as he knew, he didn't have any maternal family.

Eddy finally came upstairs after about ten minutes. Before he and Jimmy could leave, Mr. Johnson asked Jimmy for his autograph after he went to his room to get a basketball jersey with his favorite player's name on the back, J. Johnson. Eddy pleaded with his father to leave Jimmy alone, but Jimmy didn't mind signing the jersey for the old man. Mr. Johnson also joked that they could be family because they shared the same last name. Mrs. Johnson offered him a home cooked meal, but he declined and told her that he had just eaten. Jimmy left the Johnson household that day without realizing that he had just come into contact with his maternal kinfolks.

Dos Amigos

On the way to the doctor's office, Jimmy and Eddy talked more about their lives and how they grew up. He felt like Eddy's parents were the perfect couple and thought about what he would've done to grow up in a family setting like that. Jimmy was a little emotional when he was talking about his childhood. Without mentioning his mother's name, he told Eddy that she was a drug abuser and a prostitute who didn't spend much time with him when he was growing up. Although he held her dear to his heart, a part of him was angry sometimes because she wasn't around to be part of his success. He told Eddy that his mother and his neighborhood were his motivation, while his sister Nina was the enforcer. He said that whenever he saw his mother, the only thing he could think about was a way out of his neighborhood, and a life away from drugs, prostitution, and the streets all together.

Jimmy went on to tell Eddy that as much as his sister tried to shield him from his mother's business on the streets, he always knew what was up and he just never said anything. Jimmy mentioned how his mother came up to him one day to solicit a blowjob for crack, and he gave her his last ten dollars without her ever realizing that she was talking to her own son. There were things that happened with his mother that he never even told his sister, because he knew she wanted to protect him. He told Eddy how close he and Nina were, and that he would not be where he was in life without her support and strength. Eddy just listened as Jimmy talked about his childhood and upbringing. Jimmy also never failed to make Pastor Jacobs the highlight of his stellar basketball career. He didn't refer to Pastor Jacobs as his Dad, but Eddy quickly made the connection between the two.

After realizing that he had been the only one talking during the drive to the doctor's office, Jimmy stopped and apologized to Eddy for unloading all his problems on him. Eddy told him, "That's what friends are for. If I can't sit here and listen to you vent or talk about issues that bother you, then what's the point of being friends?" Eddy's statement to Jimmy was reassurance that Jimmy indeed had a true friend in Eddy. As much as Jimmy wanted to have the perfect upbringing like he thought that Eddy had, Eddy wanted to set him straight about the misconception he saw back at his house. After Jimmy made a comment about Eddy being brought up in a loving family, Eddy said to him "What's on the surface is not always what it seems." Jimmy didn't understand the comment, and he asked Eddy to elaborate. Eddy started to divulge to Jimmy how his father had allowed religion to control his life, and in the process his family had lost two of its members. Eddy could only recall waking up and not seeing his older sister in the house anymore. His father told him that his sister was sent to Upstate New York to live with relatives. He never questioned what he was told, and still believed that his sister was still alive. Before Eddy could get too far in the story they reached the doctor's office.

It's a Match!

Jimmy never got to hear Eddy's whole story, and he was nervous when he walked into the doctor's office. Whenever he came to see his doctor, the medical assistant always took time out to flirt with Jimmy. Even when Jimmy was accompanied with Lisa, she would try to flirt with him. "Some people will take their chances on lust regardless of whom they disrespect." Lisa always said. Jimmy was too worried about his future to pay any attention to the Medical Assistant's advances. He was focused on finding a kidney so he could extend his life a few more years.

Dr. Morris had become quite familiar with Jimmy over the years and he sympathized with him because he was one of the doctor's favorite patients. Jimmy had inherited his father's infectious personality, and there was a silent campaign to help find him a kidney. The doctor was very excited to tell Jimmy that he had about five potential donors who wanted to help him any way possible. Dr. Morris had grown fond of Jimmy because he didn't act like a spoiled millionaire like most of the other athletes he had come in contact with. Jimmy always took the time to play videogame with the Doctor's son when his son was in the office. Sometimes, it seemed like Jimmy never even had a childhood because he enjoyed the videogames just as much as the doctor's son. It was that part of his personality that everyone fell in love with.

While Jimmy was in the office talking to Dr. Morris, Eddy nervously waited in the waiting area. He had no idea what he was up against, but he sincerely wanted to help out his friend. After flipping through the pages of the numerous magazines, Eddy was relieved to find Jimmy and Dr. Morris standing in front of him moments later when he raised his head. Dr. Morris sensed that Eddy was nervous, so he tried easing his mind with straightforward honesty. He reassured him that it was going to be a rigorous process, but at the end of the procedure he would walk away fine.

Just like a scared little kid who was going to see the doctor for the first time, Eddy followed Dr. Morris to his office almost shitting bricks. The Doctor administered a few tests before deciding to draw a sample of Eddy's blood. Eddy was then taken to the transplant Nephrologist so he could administer the rest of the tests.

It would be a week before Dr. Morris received the results from the tests, and Jimmy and Eddy were impatiently waiting. Eddy did not even understand the significance of what he was about to do for Jimmy. Since Jimmy was deemed suitable for transplant he was not worried about himself, but he was hoping and praying that Eddy would be a match for him. Dr. Morris called Jimmy a few days later to explain to him a new discovery in kidney transplants, and how it would increase his chances for a donor. According to Dr. Morris, "To increase the possibilities for organ donation, the Center used new clinical protocols that made it possible to transplant kidneys across different blood types." Jimmy was very happy to hear that his chances for a transplant would increase. He went on about his life and he prayed to God everyday for an answer. Pastor Jacobs held special prayers at the church for Jimmy and deep down in his heart, he knew that the Lord was gonna find a way to keep his boy alive.

A week passed and Dr. Morris called Jimmy with the good news that Eddy was a perfect match. Jimmy was speechless on the phone for almost five minutes. Dr. Morris thought he had passed out for a moment, but when Jimmy screamed aloud, "Praise the Lord!" through the phone, Dr. Morris was assured that he was still alive and well. Everyone was happy for Jimmy, but he had to call his savior, Eddy, to tell him that he was a perfect match. Eddy was overjoyed with the news and he wanted to get the operation out of the way as soon as possible.

The Surgery

Since Eddy was determined a good match, Dr. Morris scheduled surgery immediately. Jimmy's family stayed at the hospital the whole time he was in surgery. His wife, Lisa, was restless as she silently prayed for her husband to make it out of the operating room alive. Even though Dr. Morris had tried his best to ease Lisa's worries, she couldn't contain herself. The surgery took almost five hours. A board-certified surgeon performed the operation successfully. After the operation, Eddy and Jimmy were taken to the Post Anesthesia Care Unit where they received state-of-the-art monitoring and individualized care from specially trained nursing professionals and well-trained doctors.

Eddy never even told his parents about the good deed that he was doing for Jimmy. Eddy knew that his father's selfish ways and attitude might have interfered with a decision that was all his own. Eddy didn't want his dad to talk him out of doing what he wanted to do for Jimmy, so he waited until after it was done to call and tell them that he was in the hospital. Mrs. Johnson rushed to see him and brought him a home cooked meal. She also commended her son for having a great heart, and she told him she was proud of his gesture.

Both, Jimmy and Eddy remained at the hospital for six days, and the doctors tried their best to show Jimmy and Lisa how to care for his new kidney. Nina was also very involved in the after-care of her brother. She stopped by the hospital everyday to make sure he was okay. Jimmy had requested to share a room with Eddy at the hospital, and over the course of six days the two families became acquainted. They mostly discussed Eddy and his big heart. Pastor Jacobs also came to the hospital everyday to see Jimmy and Eddy. Mrs. Johnson was drawn to Pastor Jacobs almost instantly at the hospital, and she promised to visit his church the upcoming Sunday.

Mrs. Johnson, Nina, Lisa, and Pastor Jacobs were all trained by the nurses at the hospital on how to care for Eddy and Jimmy. The guys were treated like babies during their stay in the hospital. Mr. Johnson never even bothered to come by the hospital to see Eddy, because he thought what Eddy did was foolish. He told Eddy that there was no guarantee that one of his kidneys wouldn't go bad and questioned why he would give one of them up. Eddy expected his dad to have a negative attitude about what he did, but he never thought that his dad would be a total ass about it.

Jimmy decided to leave the hospital early, because he didn't want the press to start hounding him daily. Eddy didn't want the media to find out who he was, because of his good deed. The media had nothing but praise for him even though they had never seen him. Jimmy showed his gratitude when he offered to buy Eddy a home of his choice anywhere in Massachusetts. Although no amount of money could have saved Jimmy's life, he felt the need to compensate Eddy for helping him. Eddy; however, graciously declined Jimmy's offer. He knew that the media would quickly conclude that his intention was to be an organ seller instead of a donor.

Staying Healthy

Before Jimmy and Eddy were discharged from the hospital, Dr. Morris stressed the fact that Jimmy had to commit to a healthy lifestyle in order for him to prosper with his new kidney. Jimmy was to follow up with the hospital regularly to ensure proper care, and to lower the risks of side effects from prescribed medication and kidney rejection. The doctors wanted to make sure that the risk of infection was minimized so that Jimmy's body could withstand the new kidney.

It was also explained to Jimmy that he ran a greater risk of high blood pressure, diabetes, high cholesterol, and a certain form of cancer after his transplant. It was made clear to him that he had to adapt to his new lifestyle because a transplant is not a cure, but a treatment for kidney failure. Treatment for Jimmy's kidney would be a lifelong process in order to deal with the different elements of the treatment plan.

As an athlete, Jimmy was already committed to a life of exercise, but he needed to develop a healthier diet than he was used to prior to his transplant. Eddy also joked that Jimmy had better not abused his body or he would take back his kidney. Maintaining good health was not an issue for Jimmy, because he was not a smoker and he didn't indulge in alcohol. Jimmy would no longer be able to sit in the sun by his pool, however, because overexposure in the sun could negatively affect his health.

The complications were less risky for Eddy as a donor. He wouldn't have much physical adjustment, but he had to watch his diet and exercise regularly as well. He and Jimmy made a pact to develop an exercise regimen that they could both enjoy. During the recovery period, Jimmy and Eddy developed a bond like brothers. They kept their doctor appointments together, and they managed to keep an exercise schedule that was suitable for both of them.

The surgery forced Jimmy to sit out the upcoming season and Eddy took a six-month leave of absence from his job. The doctors at the hospital didn't want to scare Jimmy, but they had to inform him that the national statistical average survival rate for kidney transplants from a live-donor was twenty one to twenty two years. Jimmy had a higher rate of survival, because Eddy was an exact genetic match.

Nina was so concerned about her brother's health. She absorbed as much information about kidney transplants as she could from the website www.ustransplant.org. Nina knew that education was the key to keeping her brother healthy. She also brought home as much information as she could from the library for Lisa to make sure that she was aware of everything as well. Jimmy's recovery went pretty smooth, and he was given the green light to return back to basketball a year after his transplant.

Becoming An Organ Donor

While going through their ordeal, Jimmy, Nina, and Lisa found out through research how uninvolved African Americans were regarding organ donations. Yet, African Americans suffered the most from kidney failure. After Jimmy's recovery, the whole family decided to sign up as organ donors. They saw the need and they took action. Had Eddy not sacrificed his own organ to help Jimmy, no one knew how long he would have survived on a failing kidney. Jimmy was more than happy to sign-up, because he knew that extending someone else's life in need would be the only thing he could do to show true gratitude.

Pastor Jacobs and the rest of the clan signed up as well when they learned the statistics for African-Americans and the chances of survival through organ donation. They felt very ignorant about their lack of knowledge about organ donation. If Jimmy had never gone into the hospital for his surgery, they would have never known about the need for bone marrow transplants, kidney transplants, blood transfusions, and many other illnesses that African Americans suffer that they could collectively help their community fight.

The family was also very weary of the myth: "If one of them was involved in a serious a car accident, the hospital would most likely allow them to die in order to use an organ from them to save someone else." That myth keeps many people from becoming organ donors, not just in African-American communities, but in all communities.

Reconnecting With Family

As Jimmy and Eddy grew closer as friends, certain subjects could not be ignored. Eddy never really got the chance to finish his conversation about his two missing sisters with Jimmy prior to the transplant. It was something that bothered Eddy since Karen went missing. He never before had a buddy like Jimmy, and he could not talk to his parents because he felt they were responsible for the loss of his sisters. One day while they were working out, Eddy asked Jimmy about his mother. In the past Jimmy had kept his mother a secret, because he didn't want anybody running to the press with his mother's story. Since he and Eddy were practically connected at the kidney, he told Eddy that his mother had committed suicide when he was a little boy and he didn't know much about her because she was on drugs most of the time when she was alive.

Eddy saw the pain in Jimmy's eyes, and he could feel the pain in Jimmy's heart as he revealed the story. Eddy asked what his mother's name was and Jimmy told him Katrina. After Jimmy told him his mother's name, Eddy thought about it for a few seconds. He shook his head as if to say it would be an impossible coincidence. Jimmy wanted to know why he shook his head the way he did. Eddy told him that his oldest sister's name was Katrina, and that she had left home when she was fourteen years old. They never heard from her after she left. The description that Jimmy gave of Katrina was not the same description that Eddy remembered. Eddy was only seven years old when Katrina left and because the family hadn't taken many pictures; he could only remember Katrina the way she was in her last picture with the family when she was twelve years old.

It felt a little strange to both of them that they were both connected to someone named Katrina Johnson. Jimmy's inquiring mind wanted to know more. He asked Eddy if he wouldn't mind coming over to Nina's house to talk more about his sister. Eddy said, "It would be my pleasure." Jimmy picked up his cell phone and called his sister to tell her that he wanted to come by with Eddy to talk about something very important. She told him "No problem. By the time you get to the house I will have dinner ready." Collin had not yet gotten home when Jimmy spoke with Nina. He would show up at the house with his friend and best man, John O'Malley, later.

O'Malley loved to go over to Collin's house because he enjoyed Nina's cooking. He knew that since Nina was suspended from the force she was home everyday and she cooked almost all the time. Jimmy and Eddy arrived at the house first and Collin and O'Malley showed up a half an hour later. Before anything was ever discussed Nina had the table set with food because she knew her husband was on his way home and she wanted everyone to eat together. She wasn't expecting John, but she was not surprised that he showed up. Collin had called his wife earlier to make sure she was cooking and whenever he did that, Nina knew John would show up at the house with him.

That day Nina went all out with the meal, because she was expecting a new face to come eat at her house. It was also her way of thanking Eddy for saving her brother's life. Nina's children were sitting next to their mother at the table so she could monitor them. Nina was some kind of woman. She had slaved over the stove all day while watching her children. She had to make sure that they were entertained. She read to them, bathed them, fed and monitored them while she was cooking. Sometimes, her

131

husband wondered where she got the strength or even the talent to do all these things simultaneously. He showed appreciation by doing the little things for her that most kind hearted women would appreciate. It was not unusual for Collin to come home to rub her feet, give her a bath, or just take her to a spa for the day to pamper her. She received flowers regularly from her husband, and he never went to bed without telling her how much he loved her.

While everyone was sitting at the table eating, John O'Malley who had not formally met the adult Eddy yet noticed something familiar about him. Collin pointed out the fact that Eddy was the man who donated the kidney to Jimmy. John was staring at Eddy for a different reason, however. He had seen Eddy before, a long time ago in Hyde Park, when his sister Karen was reported missing by his parents. John had the case when it was first opened, but it was transferred to another officer and still remained open with the Boston Police Department. John asked Eddy if he had a sister named Karen who went missing a few years ago. Eddy answered "Karen has never been found." John had gotten pretty close to Eddy's family, and he remembered his mother saying that she had not seen her oldest daughter, Katrina, in years as well. John also asked, "Did your other sister ever go back home?" Eddy answered "No."

The topic was now open for discussion. That is when Jimmy told Nina that Eddy had a sister named Katrina who left home at a very young age and he was wondering whether there was a possible link to his mother and Eddy's sister, Katrina. Other than the obvious first and last names, there was no other connection between Katrina that they knew of. It was fine to have this coincidence with Katrina, but it was rare that Jimmy and Eddy shared the same blood type as stated by the doctors at the hospital. Jimmy and Nina were getting excited about the possibility of discovering their family. The more they spoke to Eddy about Katrina, the more they were convinced it wasn't a coincidence.

As police officers, even John and Collin knew that there were too many pieces connected to that puzzle. The fact that Eddy told them that his sister left home at fourteen years old almost confirmed that they were, indeed, related. Eddy could not tell Jimmy and Nina that his sister was pregnant when she left home, because his parents had kept that a secret from him. They were starting to connect the dots. The only thing left to do was to set up a meeting with Eddy's parents to find out if their mother was pregnant when she left home. Eddy was also sad to hear that his possible sister had committed suicide, and that he never really got a chance to know her. At least, he knew then that his sister was resting in heaven and that was a form of closure for him. Eddy was almost certain that his sister Katrina was the same woman who gave birth to Nina and Jimmy.

Everyone was excited about the prospect of Nina and Jimmy discovering their long lost family. Even John got involved in the "tear shedding" at the table. Collin was very happy that his wife was finally going to discover her roots, because it had long been bothering her. She wanted so much to accept her husband, Pastor Jacobs, and Jimmy as her only family, but she wasn't totally satisfied without her complete family. Collin could see the joy in his wife's face after she learned the possibility of discovering her kinfolks.

Eddy was excited as well. He couldn't believe that he had been interacting with his own nephew this whole time without knowing it. He picked up the phone and called his mother to arrange a dinner at her house with Jimmy, Nina, and her family. Mrs. Johnson had seen Nina and Jimmy at the hospital when she visited her son, but they didn't really get too chatty with one another. Eddy didn't even tell his mother what the dinner was about. He simply told his mother that he wanted to celebrate life with his friends and family, and asked if she could cook his favorite meals. His mother and father hadn't done anything remotely enjoyable since Karen was gone, and Eddy wanted to foster change in their lives.

A Family Connection

A dinner was scheduled for 6:00 pm on Sunday evening. Mrs. Johnson was very excited about hosting a dinner party at her house for a celebrity athlete. Unbeknownst to her was the fact that this athlete was possibly her grandson. Everyone showed up on time, but Mrs. Johnson had anticipated for some of the guests to be late. Dinner wasn't quite ready when Jimmy, Lisa, Nina, Collin, their two children, and Pastor Jacobs showed up at the house. Everyone got reacquainted with each other and Mr. Johnson introduced himself for the first time to the clan. Eddie and Mr. Johnson played host until Mrs. Johnson got dinner ready. Mr. Johnson was enthralled by the presence of a star athlete in his home and that was the only reason he took part in the dinner.

While everyone waited in the living room, Jimmy and Nina looked through the family's photo album, and in it they saw plenty of pictures of their mother. Nina recognized her mother almost instantly as she flipped through the pages of the photo album, her eyes were getting teary. She started reminiscing about all the times her mother was struggling to keep her head above water. A part of Nina resented being at the Johnson's house, because she knew that even though her mother didn't tell her much about her grandparents that they were somewhat responsible for her downfall. A feeling of uneasiness came over her. Her husband Collin noticed the change in his wife's composure. He went over to her and placed his arms around her for comfort. She whispered to him that she didn't think she could go through with telling these people that she was their granddaughter.

Although Collin wanted to support his wife's decision, he also felt that it was necessary for her to learn about her family heritage. He called Jimmy over so they could talk to Nina and show support. Mr. Johnson had no idea what was going on between Nina and Jimmy. Eddie was busy playing with Nina's two children while Mr. Johnson talked Lisa's ear off. Every little wrinkle on Mr. Johnson's face that day said something to Nina and none of it was pleasant. She could see a callous man who had not a clue about anything, but thought he was in charge of everything. It seemed like he was forcing his antisocial behind to take part in this dinner, and they could all sense it. Mrs. Johnson, however, was very pleasant and kept checking on everybody while the food was being prepared.

Mrs. Johnson reminded Nina of her mother, and she took the opportunity to offer her help in the kitchen so she could get to know her grandmother better. When Nina went back to the kitchen, she didn't expect Mrs. Johnson to drop a load on her. Mrs. Johnson was teary eyed as she told Nina her wish of having a happy family that consisted of her children and grandchildren. She went on to tell Nina some of the hidden family secrets about her two missing daughters. Mrs. Johnson felt comfortable enough with Nina to open up to her right away. After listening to Mrs. Johnson divulged some of her family's deepest secrets, Nina knew there was no turning back. She was talking to a woman who had longed to see her missing daughters, and was very resentful of her stubborn husband whom she almost allowed to destroy her family completely.

Mrs. Johnson didn't have to tell Nina that her husband was stubborn and sometimes ignorant. She was able to read right through the man from the little time that she had spent with him in the living room. Nina knew that Mrs. Johnson was probably not responsible for the hard life that her mother had led on the streets. She felt that Mrs. Johnson could have been the voice of reason and at least tried to reach out to her daughter, however. Though sympathetic, Nina wasn't completely forgiving. She stood there in the kitchen playing the scene in her head where she would reveal to Mrs. Johnson that she was her granddaughter. She imagined laughter and happiness on Mrs. Johnson's part, but she couldn't see Mr. Johnson as a welcoming grandfather. The man seemed too miserable to be happy about anything.

The food was almost ready. Mrs. Johnson asked Nina to return to the living room while she set the dining room table and put everything together to serve her guests. First, she gave Nina a hug and thanked her for listening to her pain. Nina told her it was a pleasure and not to worry about it. Nina walked back to the living room and found Jimmy and her husband fully engaged in a conversation with Eddy and Mr. Johnson about the Patriots while watching a football game on television. Mr. Johnson was talking about the obvious racism that clouded the city of Boston when it came to their African American athletes. Mr. Johnson emphasized the fact that the sports organizations in New England are always looking for a white superstar represent their teams. He also discussed the fact that a great quarterback like Donovan McNabb or Michael Vick would have never been given the opportunity to start for the Patriots regardless of their talent.

Jimmy saw something in his grandfather that he also possessed. Mr. Johnson had a fire and determination in him to succeed at all costs, despite the odds. He wanted to prove to people, or specifically to white people, that he was just as good as they were. Perhaps, it was that determination and fire that drove him to push his daughter out of his life because he was ashamed of her for some reason. Jimmy was determined and fiery, but he was not living for anybody other than himself. He didn't care much about what white people thought of him, he simply wanted to take care of his family and help those less fortunate in his community. Collin also took part in the conversation and brought up the fact that the Boston Police Department had suspended his wife, because she wasn't making enough arrests and didn't write enough tickets. "Sure, they said there was no quota for arrests and tickets written in stone anywhere, but it was understood that the police officers had to make a certain amount of arrests once they were walking the beat on the street, especially in the hood," Collin stated.

Nina was a little idealistic in her views of community policing. She did not see the need to antagonize young black males just so she could take them to jail, creating a barrier against their future. She was getting tired of watching the white officers go into the black community, and harass the young black males. When these young men reacted to the maltreatment or harassment, they usually found themselves in the back of a police cruiser being taken to the police station to be processed on trumped-up charges that were fabricated by the police officers. Nina knew what it was like in her neighborhood and she wanted to educate people first before arresting them. Half the young black males in the hood didn't know or understand the significance of a police arrest record. They heard stories of people glorifying the fact that they had been to jail, but they didn't see the doors being shut down on them as adults looking for work because of a criminal record.

Nina was aware of the fact that most of the times, these felons couldn't even get a break to get started in life. When the time came for them to start a family of their own, they would sometimes become desperate and have to resort to selling drugs or committing other criminal acts in order to provide for their families. As a police officer on the side of the law, Collin highlighted those points as well to make sure that Eddy and Jimmy understood their stance in society with the police. He also stressed that ninety percent of the time that the judges went with the police officers' accounts of events because they're both on the side of the law. No amount of money or star status could keep a black man from being arrested for no reason at all. He gave a great example of this when Dee Brown, the former Boston Celtics player, was arrested in Wellesley while waiting in his car for his wife. He was guilty of a crime until proven innocent and the crime he committed was driving around in a BMW in Black skin in a white neighborhood.

While Nina stood in the doorway listening to her husband defending her honor, Mrs. Johnson came to the living room to announce that dinner was served. Nina gleefully smiled at her husband as she made her way to the dining room behind Mrs. Johnson. Everyone followed to the dining room promptly after. Mr. Johnson was seated at the head of the table while Mrs. Johnson sat on the other end. Eddy was all smiles, because he was about to reveal the happiest news to his family.

Everyone found some of the best tasting southern fried chicken, collard greens, black-eyed peas, macaroni and cheese, white rice, corn bread, and Kool-aid prepared by Mrs. Johnson in the dining room that day. The mood was quite festive. Mrs. Johnson wanted to treasure every moment in the presence of her new friends. She knew that once they left, she would revert back to her old ways with her husband and she would be sad all over again. However, this time she would find out news that she never expected.

Before anybody could dig into the serving bowls to fill up their plates, Pastor Jacobs asked them to bow their heads in prayer. The food smelled so good it ended up being the shortest prayer known to mankind. Everyone loved Mrs. Johnson's cooking and Nina's children kept comparing Mrs. Johnson's food to their mother's. Every time they made a comment about their mother being just as good a cook as Mrs. Johnson, Collin shook his head, because he knew that Nina was not as great a cook as her grandmother, however, she was good. Mrs. Johnson encouraged everyone to eat as much as they could because she didn't cook like that very often. Mrs. Johnson fed Nina's children like they were her own grandchildren and they kept asking her if she was their Grandma. Little did Mrs. Johnson know, she was about to find out that she was a Grandma and Great-Grandma that day.

Finally, after everyone finished their food, Nina asked to have everyone's attention because she had something important to say to the family. As everyone quieted down to allow the food to digest, Nina commenced speaking "I never thought that this day would ever come. My brother and I always dreamt about this special day and through the grace of God and the kindness of someone we thought at first, was a complete stranger to us, made being here today possible. Jimmy and I went through a lot as children because our mother neglected us and most of the time we didn't know where our next meal was going to come from."

Nina continued as she pointed to Pastor Jacobs, "God didn't just bless my brother and I once; he blessed us many times over. One of those times was when he brought Pastor Jacobs into our lives. I know that we have never formally thanked him for all that he has done for us, but we want him to know today that we love him from the bottom of our hearts, and he's the only father that we have known. But, today is another blessed day for us. We have finally found our maternal family with the help of Eddy who's not only my brother's lifesaver and angel, but also a great friend and newly found uncle to him. When I was looking through the photo album in the living room, I fought back tears as I reminisced about the good times that my mother shared with us. After spending time in the kitchen with Mrs. Johnson, I realized that my mother inherited her affectionate ways from her. So without further ado and more rambling from me, I just want to tell Mr. and Mrs. Johnson that we are your grandchildren and your daughter Katrina was our mother."

The room fell silent for a brief moment after Nina revealed that she was part of the Johnson family. Mrs. Johnson had long thought that she would never again in her life reconnect with her daughter, Katrina. She had given up hope and wondered what became of her daughter. Of course, the next question out of Mrs. Johnson's mouth was "Where's Katrina?" with great anticipation. The room was about to become silent once again and the joyous emotion that lived there momentarily was about to be replaced with anger, pain, hatred, and feelings of loss. Since Nina had delivered the good news, Jimmy took it upon himself to tell Mr. and Mrs. Johnson that Katrina passed long ago when they were teenagers. She was in Heaven somewhere watching over her family.

Throughout the whole announcement, Mr. Johnson didn't show any emotion at all. It was as if this man was emotionless and didn't care if people saw his inhumane side. But Mrs. Johnson ran towards her grandchildren and tried to spread her arms around them as much as she could to hug them as she broke down in tears at the news that her daughter was dead. Eddy tried to comfort his mother, but his father remained stoic in his seat without saying a word. It was almost like the old man had forgotten that he ever had a daughter named Katrina. Nina's children were trying to hug their mother, asking her if she was all right. Collin took them away to give Nina and Jimmy time to embrace their Grandmother and Eddy.

The lack of emotion from Mr. Johnson angered Lisa and Collin, and they both wanted to say something on behalf of their spouses. Before Lisa could open her mouth to say something to Mr. Johnson Collin reminded her that she was in his house and disrespecting him would only be stooping to his level. While Jimmy, Nina, Eddy, and Mrs. Johnson mourned Katrina's death all over again in the dining room, Mr. Johnson got up from his chair and went to his bedroom. He didn't say anything to anybody and nobody paid him any mind. Perhaps that was his way of mourning.

The family realized that day how hard it was to bring someone out of darkness who chose to remain there. Mr. Johnson's action only reassured his wife that his ignorance was almost beyond repair. She was happy to meet her grandchildren, but she was angry that she had to remain in that house to continue to live with her husband. The sight of him was making her and Eddy sick to their stomachs. Nina and Jimmy didn't particularly care for him either. They were satisfied for having found their uncle and grandmother. Mrs. Johnson also informed them about their aunt, Karen, whom had been missing for years. She noted that they couldn't find her, because they lacked the financial resources to offer a reward for information leading to her whereabouts.

Jimmy wished he had met his family a long time ago, because he would have put up a reward for Karen from the moment she disappeared. He promised his grandmother that he would do all that he could to help locate Karen's body so she could have closure. Nina shook her head in agreement as she told her grandmother that she would ask her husband to put the word out on the streets again about Karen. Mrs. Johnson ended up having one of the most joyous days since she last saw her daughter, Katrina.

Getting to Know the Family

It had been a few months since Jimmy and Nina found their maternal grandparents, and everything was going well with the family. Nina and Jimmy tried as much as they could to catch up, and make-up for the time they'd missed with their grandmother. Nina's two children, Katrina and Collin Jr., enjoyed being spoiled by their great-grandmother. Mrs. Johnson especially spoiled Katrina, because she was named after her daughter. Little Katrina shared a few similar traits with her grandmother, Katrina as well.

Jimmy had asked his uncle, Eddy, to resign from his position as a custodian with the Boston Celtics and to begin working for him as an Assistant Director to Pastor Jacobs with his nonprofit after-school program for disadvantaged youths. Eddy had always been an intelligent man, but because he didn't know how to deal with the loss of his two sisters he never maximized his potential. He was a quick learner under the tutelage of Pastor Jacobs. Eddy learned the functions of his new job in no time, and he became one of the favorite staff members to the kids. Jimmy also helped Eddy with the purchase of his first home. Jimmy's story had lost interest in the media, and he was glad because he wanted to spend the time to get to know his family.

Since Eddy bought his home, Mrs. Johnson spent very little time in the house with her husband, because she was miserable there. Nina and Collin had finished the basement in their home and they turned it into an in-law apartment for Mrs. Johnson and she spent a lot of time there getting to know Nina, Collin, and their children. She didn't want to spend too much time around a grumpy, miserable, old man. Mr. and Mrs. Johnson were too old to even bother filing for divorce, even though they couldn't stand each other. Things became very tense in the house, especially after they both retired. Even though there were hardly any words spoken, the tension in the house was at an all time high. Mrs. Johnson started to resent doing everything for a man who didn't want to treat her with respect and didn't show her any appreciation.

Nina and Collin could sense how unhappy Mrs. Johnson was in the house every time they visited with her. When they offered to remodel their basement so she could spend more time at their house with them and the children, Mrs. Johnson jumped at the opportunity to get away from her husband. Meanwhile, Nina and the Boston Police Department had reached a lucrative settlement for her unjust termination, and she decided to resign altogether from her job to become a homemaker. During that time she was also trying to get pregnant with her third child, and having her Grandmother in the house with her eased the burden a little with the other two children.

Mr. Johnson was as grumpy as ever, but this time there was no one in the house for him to take out his frustrations. He would sit in front of the television all day to watch sports, and would only step out on his porch to grab his newspaper and mail. For the sake of Jimmy and Nina, Pastor Jacobs would occasionally stop by Mr. Johnson's house to see how he was doing. He also tried to get him to open up about some of the issues that were bothering him. Pastor Jacobs would visit the old man for hours and he wouldn't exchange but a few sentences with Pastor Jacobs during the visits. Those few sentences were the usual greetings such as "how are you?" or "What brings you to my neck of the woods today?" Pastor Jacobs knew whatever it was that kept Mr. Johnson from expressing his feelings to his family had to be dealt with, and only a professional psychologist could get him to talk about his feelings.

One day during a visit at Mr. Johnson's house, Pastor Jacobs asked Mr. Johnson how he would feel about seeing a specialist about the loss of his two daughters. Surprisingly, Mr. Johnson was open to the idea. Even though it was little progress, Pastor Jacobs was happy to report to Jimmy and Nina that their grandfather had agreed to see a psychologist about his issues. Of course, Jimmy offered to pay for the sessions. Pastor Jacobs scheduled the first appointment as soon as he could before the old man changed his mind. Jimmy also agreed to pick up his grandfather to bring him back and forth to the doctor's office for his appointments. It was his way of trying to connect with the old man.

Breaking Down the Wall of Silence

As much as Jimmy wanted to ignore his grandfather for being ignorant and stubborn, it was bothering him deep down in his heart that his grandfather was not as loving and receptive as his grandmother. He wanted to break through the old man to show him that he didn't have to be so mean and emotionless all the time. It almost seemed like the days of working in the cotton fields never ended for Mr. Johnson. The man did not know how to be happy and he did not want to embrace happiness. Jimmy would have none of it. Jimmy was planning to have children with his wife, and he wanted them to know their Great-Grandfather, because he had experienced what it was like to live without knowing his whole family.

Jimmy was very sympathetic towards his grandfather and he wanted to see a better side of him. While the rest of the family was all but eager to abandon the old man, Jimmy wanted to try a little harder. He felt that the old man gave everyone the cold shoulder because he felt like he had failed Katrina. He thought, with enough effort and encouragement, everyone would find the good in the old man. Even Mrs. Johnson had never gotten the better side of the old man during their entire marriage. Jimmy wanted to see his family together and happy, and the only person standing in the way of complete happiness was Mr. Johnson. He had to be dealt with.

When Jimmy picked up Mr. Johnson for the first time for his appointment with the doctor, the old man almost changed his mind. He thought that the doctor would label him a lunatic just like the family had thought of him. He told Jimmy "I know that I agreed to see this shrimp, but I'm not gonna let nobody tell me that I'm crazy, because I

147

ain't." Jimmy had to correct his grandfather and told him that the proper term was "shrink". His grandfather responded "Shrimp or shrink, they're all the same to me. They all like to tell people how crazy they are." That was the most words Mr. Johnson had spoken since Jimmy met him and Jimmy knew that there was another side to this man. He just sat back in the car and smiled at his grandfather's confusion of the word.

When they finally made it upstairs to the Psychologist's office, Jimmy asked his grandfather if he wanted him to come in with him for support. Mr. Johnson told him "I ain't afraid of nobody. I can take on this shrimp by myself. He just better not tell me I'm crazy." The doctor came out to greet Jimmy and his grandfather, but before he brought him into his office Jimmy asked if he could have a word with him. Jimmy explained to the doctor the circumstances in his grandfather's life such as the loss of his daughters and the discovery of his new family. The doctor shook Jimmy's hand and assured him that he would take great care of his grandfather.

The doctor asked Mr. Johnson to walk inside his office in front of him. Mr. Johnson answered, "Why I gotta walk in front of you? Are you planning to stick a knife on my back or something? It's your office, you should go in first." He turned to Jimmy and said "Don't never let nobody walk behind you because you don't know who's gonna stab you in the back." As Jimmy made his way out to the lobby, the doctor turned to Mr. Johnson and told him "Nobody's going to stab you Mr. Johnson. I'm here to help you." Mr. Johnson responded "I know you ain't gonna stab me, because you want me to stab you, so you can say I'm crazy. But I ain't gonna stab you either. I just want to get to know my grandchildren and my great grandchildren. Can you tell me how to go about doing that, doc?" The doctor suddenly keyed in on the fact that Mr. Johnson was interested in getting to know his family better. It was an opening that the doctor was praying for and Mr. Johnson brought it right to him. The doctor locked the door behind him as Mr. Johnson took a seat on the couch in his office.

Mr. Johnson came out of the psychologist's office a couple hours later, acting like a new man. He was so talkative during the ride home Jimmy wanted to drown out his voice with the radio. Mr. Johnson wouldn't let him. The old man was talking about things that Jimmy had no idea about. He started telling Jimmy about the time when he met his wife and how they fell in love, how he always wanted the best for his family, and the great joy that Katrina brought him and his wife when she was born. The old man went on and on in the car. As annoying as he might've been, Jimmy knew that it was a huge breakthrough for the family. The doctor had scheduled two more appointments to see the old man during the week. He would subsequently see the old man twice a week for the next three months until the old man learned how to express his feelings of loss and guilt to his family. Mr. Johnson pulled out a treatment plan and a schedule from his back pocket, and handed it to Jimmy. Jimmy was surprised at the progress that his grand-daddy had made after just one visit.

He was excited about seeing the doctor, but most importantly he was excited about the possibility of winning his wife and family over again. Mr. Johnson was learning to grieve the best way he could, and the doctor encouraged his rambling during their session. That was the type of therapy that worked for him. The doctor would speak to Jimmy every time he brought his grandfather to the hospital and update him on his progress. The old man was slowly coming around. He was starting to do more things outside of the house, and he even suggested that he and Jimmy see a movie together. Jimmy was most pleased at the suggestion. As mean spirited as Mr. Johnson was in the beginning, Jimmy learned that he was also resilient. It was perhaps from him, he and his sister had inherited that trait.

Over the next few months, Jimmy and his grandfather became very close. Mr. Johnson expressed his pain to his grandson about the way he had treated his family in the past. Most of his maltreatment stemmed from the lack of nurturing from his own father when he was growing up. Mr. Johnson had been ridden with guilt since Katrina left home, but because he wanted to stand by his decision to kick her out of the house he never went to look for her. Mr. Johnson had never before shed any tears and after learning about his harsh upbringing, Jimmy was surprised when Mr. Johnson got teary-eyed when he talked about his family. He had missed out on the formal years of his grandchildren's lives, and he didn't want to hold on to that bitterness anymore.

Meanwhile, Jimmy took every opportunity to tell his grandmother about the new changes in his grandfather. Even Nina and Lisa agreed that the old man had started to see a better way in life. Mrs. Johnson was not so easily convinced. She had been with that man for over thirty years, and she knew that no psychologist could help change him that significantly in such a short amount of time. She still wanted nothing to do with him. It would take Jimmy, Nina, Lisa, and Collin to try to persuade Mrs.

Johnson that her husband had made great strides in counseling and that he deserved a second chance.

Jimmy was starting to feel connected to his grandfather and he wanted to help him win over his wife. As much progress as the old man made, he wasn't ready to learn how to be romantic. For Mr. Johnson, love was understood not expressed. He had never learned to express love to anyone. As long as he provided for his family and protected them that was enough love from him. Jimmy would show his grandfather another way. The old man was apprehensive at first. Every time he thought about the lonely nights he spent at his house without his wife, he agreed little by little to follow Jimmy's suggestions to get his wife back.

Since Nina knew how romantic her husband was, she suggested that Jimmy talk with Collin about ways that Mr. Johnson could woo his wife back into his arms. Collin was more than willing to help. First, Mr. Johnson had to establish a way to communicate with his wife. They had not spoken in so long and there was so much to be said. Mr. Johnson thought a simple apology would have his wife running back to him. When Collin explained to him how much damage control that needed to be done; he started to realize how badly he had hurt his family.

Teaching an Old Dog New Tricks

Before any plan could be established for Mr. Johnson, he first had to learn to express himself through writing. Mr. Johnson had done a great job concealing his literacy deficiency most of his life, but Jimmy was able to pick up on it when his grandfather was adamant about him reading articles in the newspaper to him all the time. He found many excuses for not being able to read the article himself and Jimmy knew it was more than meets the eye. However, approaching such a sensitive subject with Mr. Johnson would prove more difficult than Jimmy initially thought.

The fact that Mrs. Johnson was able to obtain a college degree weighed heavily on Mr. Johnson's ego. For years he had managed to manipulate the woman into thinking that she was nothing more than a subservient wife, but she would go on to prove to him that she was more than what he thought. Jimmy could've easily used his grandmother's achievements to motivate the old man, but he knew that would only add fuel to the fire. Mr. Johnson didn't understand the value of an education because he hadn't gotten one and was able to function well in life, according to him. Never once did he realize that his ignorance had cost him his family.

Tact was the most important weapon to use to get through to the old man and Jimmy was very tactful when he brought up the fact that Black people have achieved a lot considering the fact that they were prohibited from earning an education for over four hundred years in America. "Grandpa, we probably would've been much farther in life as a people if we were allowed to learn how to read the same time as other folks," he said. "Despite

152

the setback in our timing, we have produced quite a few notable figures in society. That's also one of the reasons why I went back to school to obtain my degree in accounting. Basketball is not gonna be with me forever, but I can always use my accounting skills," he continued.

A light smile came across the old man's face, he was proud that his grandson was so intelligent, and Jimmy felt he had found his angle. "Striving to improve your skills in life is a nonstop task and you shouldn't limit your intelligence because you were deprived once upon a time. Your grand kids are looking forward to you reading to them and I think it will be great to hear a story told through the voice of their grandfather," Jimmy said. "Well Jimmy, my son, I think you make a good point. I've been stubborn my whole life because I had to hide from the world what I didn't want them to know, but now I'm a grown ass man and I can do whatever the hell I want and I'm gonna learn how to read and write to get my wife and my family back," Mr. Johnson said.

Jimmy cracked open the door that had been shut for many years and the old man didn't feel threaten at all by his approach. Jimmy came by the house with books he picked up from the library, and everyday he dedicated a couple of hours of his time while in recovery to teach his grandpa how to read and write. Mr. Johnson would go on to earn his GED and was motivated by his wife to earn a Bachelor's degree in education by the time he turned seventy. It took a little longer to earn his degree because he wanted to take his time to do it right. Mr. Johnson didn't just do it for himself, he also did it for his grandchildren and for those people who never believed that they could walk away from darkness in their lifetime.

Getting Back in the Groove

Jimmy and Collin came up with a plan for Mr. Johnson to win back his wife's love and affection. They made him agree to write her a letter everyday for a month explaining to her why he had been so callous and mean, and how he planned on showing her that he was a changed man and a new person all together. There was a theme for each day and each letter had to end with the words "I Love You." Mr. Johnson never realized how hard it was to be romantic.

In the first letter, the theme was "Asking for a moment of your time". At the top of each letter, Mr. Johnson wrote his theme and handed the letter to Jimmy to give to his wife. In his first letter, he wrote to his wife to simply ask her for a few minutes of her time. He wanted nothing more than to show her how wrong he had been most of their lives, and how right he wanted to be this time around. He went on and on about situations in the house with the kids, as well as his wife, and how he didn't act like a gentleman when he should have. He rambled on paper the same way he rambled at the Doctor's office. Mrs. Johnson instantly noticed the change in her husband from all the rambling that he had done in his letters. Mr. Johnson used to be a man of few words, but all that changed. Even though he wasn't totally literate when the letters were written, his wife was able to understand his writing and noticed the improvement.

By the time Mr. Johnson wrote his twenty-fifth letter, he was doing some serious begging for forgiveness. He had also been required to send roses to his wife everyday starting with the first day he wrote his first letter. Each bouquet was equal the amount of letters he had written.

For the first time, Mrs. Johnson felt like a teenager in love. She wondered what came over her husband. The last letter she received from Mr. Johnson, he was requesting a date with her. Jimmy had arranged for a limousine to pick up his grandfather at his house. The chauffeur was instructed to go to Nina's house to pick up his grandmother. Collin made sure that Mr. Johnson was aware of the fact that he had to get out of the limousine to hold the door open for his wife, and to have two dozen roses in his hand waiting for Mrs. Johnson.

A date was set at a nice restaurant in Boston. Mr. and Mrs. Johnson ate their favorite meals, and then they were off to an annual ball for Seniors held at the VFW hall in West Roxbury. The couple had fun dancing the whole night. Mr. Johnson held his wife like a teenager in love, and she was finally happy to have fun with her husband after over thirty years of marriage. She wished he had been so sweet, kind, and romantic when they were younger, but she was indulging in the moment. At the end of the night, Mr. Johnson wanted his wife to come back home with him, because he had Viagra on ice at the house. She declined, because she still wanted to take things one day at a time. She told her husband that she appreciated all the effort that he put forth in trying to win her over, but she wasn't going to give in so easily to him. As much as Mrs. Johnson wanted to go home and be with her husband, she stuck to her guns and stayed at Nina's house.

Mr. Johnson accepted his wife's decision and he would go on to write her love notes everyday that he woke up. The letters didn't stop coming even after Mrs. Johnson moved back into the house with her husband. They both were avid watchers of Home and Garden television. Mr.

Johnson got the idea to create a secret garden of roses especially for his wife after watching a program on Home and Garden television. She woke up everyday to find a rose on the kitchen table along with a love note from her husband.

Mr. Johnson might have missed out on the lives of Jimmy and Nina, but he more than made up for it with his great-grandchildren. Collin Jr. and his sister, Katrina were always going somewhere with their great-grandparents and that gave Nina a lot of time to spend with her husband. Collin took great care of his wife when she finally became pregnant with their third child. Collin, however, also told Nina that he wanted his children to start spending time with his parents as well. Since the Johnsons came into their lives Collin Jr. and little Katrina hadn't spent much time with their paternal grandparents. Nina had complained that they were undermining the way she disciplined her children by spoiling them every time they went over there. Collin was quick to point out that Mr. and Mrs. Johnson were doing the exact same thing and Nina made no big deal of it.

Nina was a big enough person to admit her bias and Collin was able to show her that the grandparents were doing nothing wrong by showing love to the children. It was hard for Nina to swallow this, at first, because she was never spoiled as a child. When her grandparents came around she knew that she had missed out on a lot, and that made it okay for her children to be spoiled by them. The children would split their time between the two sides of the family when Collin and Nina needed to spend time together.

After reconnecting with Jimmy and Nina, Mr. and Mrs. Johnson were interested in saying their goodbyes to their daughter Katrina. The guilt of Katrina's death hadn't disappeared from their mind and they knew that they needed closure in order to move on with their lives.

Katrina's Grave revisited

The Johnsons had never gotten a chance to say goodbye to Katrina. Even Eddy wanted to speak to his sister even though she was dead. The family made plans to go to the Longwood Cemetery to visit Katrina's grave on Memorial Day. Mr. and Mrs. Johnson, Eddy, Nina, Collin, and their two children all met at Jimmy and Lisa's house for the short drive to the cemetery. Jimmy and Nina had been visiting their mother every year on Memorial Day, and leaving fresh flowers on her grave every other week. It was an emotional scene for Mrs. Johnson, her husband, and Eddy. Mrs. Johnson was especially emotional, because she felt that she didn't do a good enough job fighting for her daughter.

Mr. Johnson was able to contain himself for only a short period as he burst out in tears, and knelt down in front of his daughter's grave to ask for forgiveness. Although he had never told his daughter how much he loved her when she was alive, he couldn't stop telling her how much he missed her and how he was an imbecile who didn't know any better. He would carry the pain of her loss with him forever. Eddy was satisfied with saying his goodbyes and thanking Katrina for bringing two beautiful children into the world that he loved dearly.

Mrs. Johnson asked for a special moment with her daughter away from everyone else. She talked to her daughter about some of the activities that they never got a chance to do together. She told her daughter that she wished she had taken the time to act like a mother instead of an obedient wife to her husband. She told her daughter that she had never forgotten about her, and that her spirit continued to live within her from the time she left home.

Most of all, she told her daughter she loved her and she was always proud of her.

The whole family left the cemetery that day teary-eyed. Lisa comforted her husband, and Collin held on to his wife the way she needed to be held. Eddy simply put his arms around his Mom and Dad as they walked away from Katrina's grave. The family went out to celebrate Katrina's life at Jimmy and Nina's favorite Chinese restaurant in Saugus, Massachussetts.

Finding Karen

Jimmy and Nina had brought closure to the Johnsons when they reconnected with their grandparents, but there was still a missing piece to the Johnson family. They also had a daughter named Karen who had been missing for years. When Karen went missing she was presumed dead, because her body had never been found and the confessed killer left a note without revealing where the body was. That situation created a whole different kind of limbo in the Johnson's household. Jimmy and Nina had never met their aunt, but they could feel both their grandparent's and Eddy's pain whenever they talked about Karen. It seemed like they had given up hope, and Karen was starting to become a painful memory like Katrina was.

Jimmy and Nina could sense that the family wasn't completely happy, despite the fact that they found each other. Mrs. Johnson remained hopeful and sad at the same time. She wasn't too optimistic after she learned that Katrina had passed. Even worse was the fact that someone had admitted to killing Karen. She resonated with the fact that Karen was dead, but the family wanted to give her a proper burial.

Jimmy hired a private investigator to help find Karen. About a week later, the investigator found out that it was never reported that a State Trooper had checked on Mike on the side of the expressway. The investigator backtracked as much as he could to figure out what Mike may have done with Karen's body. There was never any report of any bodies of a black woman turning up on any rivers in the surrounding area, and the investigator hit a brick wall with the case. He urged Jimmy to start a national campaign nationwide for Karen.

A picture of Karen when she went missing at the age of sixteen was plastered on every milk carton at every supermarket in the country for a month. At first, it was a hard sell to feature Karen as missing, because her family had been told that she was killed. Jimmy was able to convince the people from the milk company that it was worth a shot to feature his Aunt as part of the campaign even if it was just for one week. When the folks from the milk corporation agreed to feature Karen for a month on their milk cartons it was a blessing from above. The whole family kept their fingers crossed, but was ready for the worse.

Karen had been gone for so long, she would have been in her thirties and looking a lot different than she did as a teenager. An expert forensic artist tried his best to make a composite of what Karen would look like in her thirties at normal weight. Jimmy tried as much as he could to get the case exposed nationally in the media. It was unusual for a missing black woman to receive any kind of national attention on television. Jimmy used his celebrity status as he embarked on a crusade to help find his aunt's body.

Jimmy was featured on many talk shows while going through his treatment for a kidney transplant, and he took every interview opportunity to talk about his missing aunt while he was on the air. He was relentless. He continued to feed the press with his hope of returning to basketball the following year while he plugged his missing aunt to the world. Jimmy also became the spokesperson for the Kidney Foundation. He wanted to educate people about kidney failure, but most importantly he wanted to urge all people in the African American Community throughout the country to sign up as organ donors. His other crusade was to find his aunt and bring closure to his grandparents.

Blackmailed

While Jimmy was traveling around the country to raise awareness for kidney failure, he was being closely watched by an old foe. Jean, the prostitute who recognized Jimmy's voice when he unintentionally caused the death of Mr. Ferry in that hotel room a few years back, had made herself very familiar with Jimmy's scheduled television appearances. One day during a taping of a talk show in New York, Jean traveled there to be part of the live studio audience, just so she could see Jimmy. She lied to the producers and told them that Jimmy was her biggest source of inspiration when she came out of her coma from a car accident in Boston. The producers found her story moving, so they arranged a private luncheon for her to meet with Jimmy. Since Jimmy was the type of person who always tried to reach out to people, he agreed to meet with Jean for a private lunch after the show.

Lunch was set up at a nice restaurant downtown Manhattan. Jean was brought to the restaurant early to wait for Jimmy. He arrived about fifteen minutes later in a limousine. The press was barred from the lunch meeting. After about ten minutes into their meal, Jean burst out "Look, I'm not here because I'm a fan of yours. I can care less about your little kidney failure campaign and your struggles to get back to basketball." Jimmy was surprised by Jean's comment. "Who are you?" he asked. "It don't matter who I am, but I know the real person behind the mask that you're wearing," she told him. "All that fake good-guy image that you're trying to portray on television is about to be exposed unless you write me a high six figure check to make your problem go away." Jimmy didn't know what hit him. He definitely knew that he had hidden skeletons, but he never thought that they would one day catch up to him.

He tried acting ignorantly by asking her what she was talking about. Jean was very sarcastic in her tone and demeanor. "Do you suddenly have amnesia?" she asked "What are you talking about?" Jimmy answered. Jean turned to him and said, "Look, I'm the one who was lying up in that hospital for almost three years in a coma, all right? I'm the one who was suffering from amnesia, but thank God my memory came back. I know that you don't want me to blurt out to everyone in the restaurant that you were the man who stabbed Ferry that night in the motel room when I was tied up to the bed?" Jimmy didn't know how to respond to Jean. He simply asked, "How much do you want?" The possibility of going to jail ran through Jimmy's mind and he was scared. He didn't know how serious Jean was, and he didn't want to take any chances. She requested three quarters of a million dollars in the form of a certified check. Jimmy asked, "How exactly do you plan on explaining to the IRS the reason why you'd be receiving such a large amount of money from me?"

She knew that he had a point and she needed to come up with another plan. "Well then, I guess you're gonna have to give me the money in cash," she said. "Just how am I supposed to get my hand on seven hundred and fifty thousand dollars in cash?" he asked.

"You'll find a way. I'm sure you have a safe hidden somewhere with some cash for emergencies," she said. Jimmy was starting to believe that the car hit Jean a little too hard on the head, because she sounded delusional. Even though Jean posed a threat to his career and livelihood, Jimmy sensed that she wasn't bright enough to follow through with her demands.

It had taken Jean a few months to regain her memory. The only thing she was familiar with was Jimmy's voice, and the incident that took place in the hotel room the night she was with the murder victim and nothing else. She had no friends or family to report this to, and she did not even remember whom she talked to about the case. Jean almost did not believe that incident really happened. She could not remember the details of the case and the doctors at the hospital told her that she would never fully regain her memory. Jean did not know where to begin if she really wanted to report Jimmy to the authorities. The case had been closed for two years and all the records were sealed at the widow's request. But Jean tried to threaten Jimmy, anyway. She told Jimmy if he didn't give her the amount of money she asked for, she would go to the police.

Jimmy wanted some time to think about his next move, so he agreed to a payment plan with Jean. He told her that because of government regulations, he could only give her nine thousand, nine hundred, and ninety nine dollars a week so that the IRS would not question the source of the money. It sounded like a good start to Jean, but it would be a great stall for Jimmy. Jean thought she had Jimmy cornered, and she couldn't wait to start spending his money lavishly. She had planned to leave the shelter where she was staying, and move into a suite at the Westin Hotel downtown Boston. Over nine thousand dollars a week for almost seventy-six weeks could go a long way. Jean was betting on that money to start living the good life. She handed Jimmy a piece of paper with a phone number where she could be reached, and Jimmy left the restaurant after shaking Jean's hand to confirm their deal. It was almost like a hand-scripted publicity stunt the way Jimmy shook Jean's hand and gave her a hug in front of everyone. Even Hollywood couldn't have written a better script.

Cornered

Jimmy left the restaurant feeling bewildered about the whole situation. He thought about going to the police to turn himself in. That thought quickly faded when he came to the realization of spending the rest of his life in jail for defending himself and his family against a scumbag who was going around molesting and raping young children. "As many children as Patrick Ferry molested when he was alive, my life and freedom should not be on the line," he whispered to himself. There had to be a different way to deal with his problems. Giving the money to Jean wasn't an issue, but Jimmy knew that the money wasn't going to keep her away. Greed has a way of rearing its ugly head when it's least expected, and he knew that Jean would come back and ask for more money. He would always have the incident clouding over his head.

The only person Jimmy had ever confessed the incident to was Pastor Jacobs, and he needed to speak with him immediately. Jimmy left New York and rushed to get on a plane to go home to Boston. He asked his publicist to cancel all his future television appearances and interviews until further notice. While on the short plane ride to Boston, Jimmy thought about his options. He had never actually thought about murdering anybody with his bare hands, but that is exactly how he felt when he was at the restaurant with Jean. He wanted to wring her neck until there was no life left in her. As much as he was trying to be a good citizen and beat the odds of where he came from, there was always something in his way that seemed to want to pull him to the life of crime.

Jimmy had created his own destiny, and he wasn't ready to let somebody else change that for him. He knew there had to be a way to get rid of Jean, and he couldn't wait to get home to talk to the man who always helped him find a solution to his problems. That man was none other than his father, Pastor Jacobs. Jimmy relied heavily on Pastor Jacobs' guidance to get through the tough times in his life, and he never had to face anything tougher.

When Jimmy arrived at the airport, Nina was there to pick him up. He would normally leave his car parked at the airport when he went away on short trips, but he had planned a five city tour. He didn't feel comfortable leaving his car parked at the airport for too long a period. When Jimmy got in the car, he was not his normal cheery self, and Nina noticed almost immediately. Nina knew her brother and she knew that something was bothering him. He simply thanked her for picking him up, because his wife, Lisa, was attending a charity event in Boston and couldn't pick him up. Jimmy didn't say much the whole ride to his house. He was somewhere that he hadn't been in a long time and getting out was going to be harder to do this time.

Jimmy couldn't even talk to Nina about his problem because he had kept the incident a secret from her as well. She wondered why her brother was so silent, but he didn't offer an explanation. "Did something happen on your trip?" She asked. "I don't really want to talk about it Nina," he told her. Nina knew very well when to leave her brother alone. She didn't say much to him in the car during the ride. She simply left him to wallow in his mess.

After Nina dropped Jimmy off at his house, he took his luggage into the house. He then hopped in his car and drove straight to Pastor Jacobs' house. He needed guidance and this matter was more serious than any matter he has ever had to face in his life. Jimmy was going out of his mind while driving to Pastor Jacobs' house. He was hoping that Pastor Jacobs would have the solution to make his problem go away. He had come too far to let some bimbo hooker ruin his life, but he also knew that the bimbo hooker now held his future in her hands. Jimmy arrived at Pastor Jacobs' house in no time.

He rang the doorbell. When Pastor Jacobs opened the door he knew that something was wrong, because Jimmy's face was flushed. As they made their way into the living room, he asked his wife to bring Jimmy some water to calm down his nerves. Pastor Jacobs asked Jimmy to take long deep breaths to recollect his thoughts before saying anything. Pastor Jacobs was trying his best to make him feel comfortable and secure, but he had no idea about what Jimmy was about to unload on him.

After about fifteen minutes of long soothing, deep breaths and a few sips of Poland Spring Water, Jimmy was calm enough to start telling Pastor Jacobs about the re-emergence of Jean from her coma and her plan of blackmail. Pastor Jacobs sat there and listened to Jimmy. He knew that Jimmy's blood pressure was rising as he told him of Jean's demands. The first words out of Pastor Jacobs' mouth "can you find a way to stall her until I can come up with a plan?" "I might be able to stall for a little while because I told her that I will be given her about ninety nine hundred and ninety nine dollars a week," Jimmy told him. "That was good thinking on your part. I should be able to come with a plan very soon. Meanwhile, you might have to make a payment to her until my plan comes to fruition," Pastor Jacobs told Jimmy.

This was one situation where Pastor Jacobs didn't readily have the answers as easily and quickly as usual. Blackmail was new to him, and he didn't want to offer any quick solutions. Jimmy's livelihood was dependent upon his plan. He asked Jimmy if he had a way of contacting Jean, and Jimmy handed him a phone number. He took the number in his hand and looked at it for a few seconds. He shook his head and wondered why this chick had to come and mess up something that was going so well. Pastor Jacobs told Jimmy to go home and not to say anything to anybody. Being a pastor took a backseat to his son, it was time for him to revert to his old street ways to get Jimmy out of trouble.

The Plan

After Jimmy left Pastor Jacobs' house, Pastor Jacobs told his wife that he would be in his office and not to bother him for a while. He pulled out the piece of paper with Jean's number from his pocket and dialed the number. A female voice answered on the other end and said, "Kind Street Inn, may I help you?" Pastor Jacobs quickly told her he had the wrong number. Pastor Jacobs knew that he recognized the number when he saw it, but he wanted to make sure. He had done some volunteer work at the Kind Street Inn Shelter and had a few contacts there in that shelter. Pastor Jacobs' plan to help his son out of the situation was suddenly getting clearer and easier.

He figured that Jean did not really have a leg to stand on as far as her story against Jimmy, so he had to find a way to expose her before she exposed Jimmy. The lure of prostitution was the only way that Jean knew how to make a living. The shelter did not allow prostitutes to take their well-deserved beds. If Jean thought she could blackmail Jimmy, Pastor Jacobs wanted to show her that two could play that game.

He did some background work and found out that Jean had only been at the shelter for a week. She was used to a certain lifestyle and with all the restrictions at the shelter; he knew that she wouldn't be able to stay there much longer due to all of the restrictions. It was a matter of time before Jean would find her way back to the streets to begin prostituting herself again. Pastor Jacobs was patiently waiting. He had come too far with his son to allow someone to destroy all his life's work. Pastor Jacobs had only one son, and he was not ready to lose him to the penal system. Anybody who got in his way was going to be dealt with whether he was a man of the cloth or not.

A Teenage Girl and a Dream

While Jimmy was going through his ordeal in Boston, far across the country there was a beautiful woman who had lost her memory due to a blow to the head. She had received this blow at the hands of an angry young man when she was just sixteen years old. A wealthy widow who always dreamed of having a child found this young woman. While taking a leisurely walk through the woods of New Hampshire, this lady came upon the hidden young woman's unconscious body breathing heavily in a card box. When the lady heard the young female voice groaning, she was startled at first because she didn't expect anybody to be in that part of the woods. At first, she tried to help the young lady by asking where she was from and if there was anything she could do to help. The young lady had no idea who and where she was. She didn't even know her name. She was suffering from a serious case of amnesia, and the lump on her temple was evidence that a blunt object may have hit her.

Since this young woman's disappearance only made the local news in Boston, nobody in New Hampshire had even heard of her. Unfortunately that day, she would find herself being cared for by a wealthy woman who wanted to be her mother and nothing else. Her new name would be Sonya Watson. The rich lady called herself Regina. There was no ill-will on Regina's part, but she knew that the young lady had a family somewhere. Her selfish needs prevented her from ever attempting to find the young girl's family. She decided that they were going to be a family, and she moved far across the country to California to prevent the authorities from ever finding out about her new daughter.

172

Regina took great care of Sonya, and gave her all the things that a little, poor, ghetto girl could ever have dreamed of. Regina had a big house on the hill and she was able to convince Sonya that she was her mother. She realized that the girl didn't know who she was. Sonya was somewhat suspicious of Regina, at first, because Regina was asking questions about her family. After realizing that the girl could not remember anything about her family, Regina claimed she was only playing with her and that she was her mother. Sonya, however, couldn't recall ever having Regina as a mother. When Sonya asked about her father, she was shown a picture of a man in a wedding picture with Regina. That man had died and left them all his fortune. Sonya would go on for the next fifteen years believing that Regina was her biological mother.

It was just Regina and Sonya for a while. The story was forged out of desperation, and for over fifteen years Sonya had been questioning that story. There was nothing around to remind her of her past, so she simply accepted the kind-hearted woman as her mom. Regina treated Sonya like a princess and offered her the world.

There were no family pictures when Sonya was young, and she wondered why. When she asked Regina why there were no pictures of her as a baby or a little girl, Regina told her that their house had burned down and all the pictures burned along with it. Sonya was also blamed for the fire, because Regina wanted to keep her from asking so many questions. She told Sonya that she was the reason why they lost all the pictures and other family heirlooms as a way to keep Sonya in-check with guilt. Regina genuinely loved Sonya and it was a perfect situation for her when she found Sonya. Regina never liked little or young kids, she wanted to have a daughter who was about fourteen years old because she didn't have the patience for younger kids. She was even a foster parent at one point in her life. Her door was always open when the Department of Social Services needed a placement for their foster teenagers. It was good for a while, but none of the girls Regina took in wanted to be adopted. She started to lose her patience with them. She stopped being a foster parent all together.

Sonya, for the most part, fulfilled a life long dream for Regina. In her own delusional and twisted ways, Regina believed that she was a great parent and that she had done a great job raising Sonya. She also made Sonya believe that her childhood was filled with happy thoughts and wonderful experiences. After all, Sonya graduated top of her class at the University of California in Los Angeles. She became a top-notch attorney and Regina was the driving force behind her success. Sonya was grateful, but she was never comfortable calling Regina mother. Regina, however, insisted on it.

Unbreakable Bonds

It was during Jimmy's tour as a spokesman for Kidney Foundation that Sonya saw him on her television screen. He was always pleading for anyone who had information regarding his aunt Karen to come forward. Jimmy also used a sketch artist to draw a picture of what Karen would look like in her thirties that he always carried in his pocket. At the end of each talk show, he would always show the picture of the young Karen and old Karen in hopes to help find her.

When Sonya saw the picture of this woman who looked so much like her, she became curious. She never knew Jimmy, so she couldn't identify with anything that he was saying. She wrote down the phone number to contact the family. Sonya's suspicions grew even more, and she wanted to confront Regina about it. She picked up the phone to call Regina and when Regina picked up she could hear the television program in the background. Regina quickly shut off the television. It was the same program that Sonya was watching, and there was something suspicious about the whole situation. Sonya demanded an explanation from Regina, but Regina wanted nothing to do with it. She told Sonya that it was figment of her imagination to even think that she was the actual woman that Jimmy had mentioned on television. Regina stepped up the guilt trip again by telling Sonya that she had been imagining things in her mind ever since the fire.

Although, Regina had provided a great life for Sonya, she always felt that she was being manipulated. Regina never wanted her to discuss anything about her family life with strangers and she was not allowed to have friends. Sonya was always leery of the woman who claimed to be her mother. Sonya had been home schooled by Regina. When she wanted to live on campus in college, Regina threw a fit and told her that she didn't want to stay in the house by herself. She bribed and convinced Sonya to stay home and commute to school by purchasing a convertible BMW for her. All those things only added to Sonya's suspicion of the woman who had possibly kidnapped her when she was a teenager. Now, she had a possible connection to her real family and Regina wanted make sure that she destroyed it.

After badgering Sonya for about ten minutes on the phone for thinking that Regina was not her mother, Sonya couldn't take it anymore because she had heard enough. She wanted to hang up on Regina. Regina became enraged and started calling Sonya an ingrate. The guilt-laden tongue-lashing she received from Regina only reinforced her belief that Regina was not her biological mother. She knew that a real mother would never consider her own daughter an ingrate. She hung up the phone before Regina could say anything more to her. After Regina heard the phone slammed down in her ear, she started cursing Sonya. She began talking to herself, "I lost a daughter already and I'm not about to lose another one," she said.

Regina had a biological daughter named Sonya who was about the same age as the Karen, whom she found in the woods. She couldn't deal with the fact that her daughter had drowned in the lake where she had discovered the girl's body, so she decided to replace her real daughter, Sonya, with the girl she found. Since Karen had forgotten who she was it was a perfect scenario for Regina. She even shaved two years off Karen's age to make her believe she was her real daughter. Regina had a birth certificate from her real daughter and she used it as proof to convince Karen that she was her daughter.

Sonya's curiosity got the best of her after she hung up the phone on Regina. She called the hotline for the number listed on the television show by Jimmy and a lady answered. "I just saw the basketball player named Jimmy on this show and I believe that I can be the missing person that his family has been looking for," she told the lady. The lady took down her name and number and promised to have Jimmy call her as soon as he could. Everything seemed surreal to Sonya at that point. She was trying to remember if people ever referred to her as Karen, but she drew a blank. Something deep inside Sonya made her feel that Regina was not biologically related to her. They looked nothing alike, and the man Regina claimed was her husband and Sonya's father also looked nothing like her.

What to do?

Sonya wrestled with the idea that she possibly grew up with a total stranger and imposter who might have taken advantage of her memory loss and kept her away from her real family. Then, she thought about the luxurious and fabulous upbringing that she had with Regina, and she decided that she didn't want to harm Regina in any way, shape or form. Regina had been nothing but loving and kind to her. Occasionally, they had their disagreements and she acted less than a mother, but for the most part, it was a loving upbringing and she was well educated and successful.

Sonya really wanted Regina to be her biological mother because of her kind heart, but the fact that she could be somebody else's child was taking over her spirit and mind. She started to feel pity for Regina, because she knew that Regina was afraid of being alone and that could have been the reason why she kept her away from her family. Sonya had no idea that Regina had actually lost a daughter. Everything in Sonya's life seemed like a fairytale. She had a caring mother, she lived in a mansion, she had a mother who stayed home to take care of her, they went on vacation around the world every summer, and she had a father who was wealthy enough to leave his family financially well-off for the next five generations. Who wouldn't want such woman to be their mother?

Sonya didn't understand her situation at all and she still had not spoken to Jimmy or the Johnson Family. She felt like she was getting ahead of herself and racking her brain to deal with a situation that she wasn't even certain about. It started taking a toll on her mentally. She decided to stop thinking about the whole situation, and just waited for the Johnson family representative to call her.

The Rescue

Although the Johnson family never gave up hope, however, they never anticipated finding Karen alive. It had been so many years and so much had happened during that time, there was no way that Karen could've possibly lived away from her family for so long, they thought. The family decided that Mrs. Johnson should place the call to Sonya. Everyone gathered in the Johnson's living room on that fateful day to find out if they had finally found Karen. Mrs. Johnson's hands were trembling as she picked up the phone to dial the number. She didn't know what kind of reaction to expect from the woman on the other end.

The phone rang three times before Sonya finally picked it up and almost instantly she recognized the voice on the other end. Sonya knew that she had heard that voice before, and it was a voice that brought joy to her when she was a little girl. Mrs. Johnson also recognized Karen's voice on the phone when she answered, "Sonya speaking." Mrs. Johnson was shocked to hear that familiar voice referring to herself as Sonya. Mrs. Johnson told her, "You sound like my baby, Karen, and there's no way that your name is Sonya." Sonya told her that her voice sounded familiar too, but she couldn't fully recall who Mrs. Johnson was. Mrs. Johnson started telling Sonya about the family she left behind in Boston, and that everyone had been agonizing over her disappearance for over a decade. She wanted to go back to the time Karen went missing, but none of it sounded familiar to Sonya.

Regina was not a stupid woman. After she found Karen, she took her to a hypnosis specialist who was able to hypnotize Karen. He made her believe that her life began at sixteen years old when she was found, and that Regina was the only family that she had. At the time, Regina told Sonya she wanted to help her remember her Dad, but under hypnosis she had other plans. Though the specialist was able to get Karen to believe that Regina was her mother, he was not able to erase her memory about her real family. He had no pictures or names to use as reference. Regina had paid the hypnotist handsomely and told him that Sonya was really her daughter.

Sonya found it strange that Mrs. Johnson had been grieving over her for so long, so she made arrangements with them to fly to Boston to meet the family the following week. Meanwhile, she continued to go by Regina's house as usual to see her and pretended that the mother-daughter relationship they had was still intact. Sonya never gave Regina any indication that she was seeking the truth about her family. When she was leaving to go to Boston, she told Regina that she was going on a short vacation to Cancun. Regina insisted on coming along, but Sonya brushed her off and told her that she needed some time alone.

Sonya arrived at the airport in Boston a week later. The whole family greeted her. Jimmy and his wife, Nina and her children, Eddy, and Mr. and Mrs. Johnson all waited at the terminal entrance for her. They didn't have to hold up any signs with Sonya's name, because Karen always shared a very close family resemblance with her mother. Eddy recognized his sister right away as he ran towards to give her a hug. She could see that he was almost a clone of her as she reluctantly hugged him back. He held her in his arms and told her how much he's been missing her and how growing up without her was unbearable. For the first time in her life, Karen recognized the family resemblance. He took her luggage and headed towards the rest of the family. Sonya was shocked to see the two people who looked most like her were standing in front of her. Mr. and Mrs. Johnson didn't want to let go of their daughter. They held her tight in a bear hug almost suffocating the young woman. She was introduced to the whole family and one by one each member of the family hugged her and told her how much she was missed.

Eddy was so overcome with joy, because he had missed his sister more than anybody. Karen and Eddy were very close when she went missing, and for the first year while she was gone, he cried himself to sleep thinking about her. His face also brought joy to her, because she could only recall good things about him. Karen kept smiling at her brother all the way home.

Karen was directed to the stretched limousine waiting outside. Once everyone was in the limo, they started pointing to her face, and the fact that her looks hadn't changed much since she was a teenager. She was still Sonya as far as she was concerned, but everyone in the car kept referring to her as Karen. Her mother and father pulled out pictures of her with the family from the time she was a baby to the time she went missing. With every picture, her memory was starting to come back to her. They showed pictures of her, Eddy, and Katrina together. It brought out different emotions from her. She recognized young Katrina and remembered that it was not a pleasant experience for her. As they were talking in the car, Mrs. Johnson told Karen that she kept her room the same way she left it before she went missing. She also stated that it would be nice to have her back in her room again. To their dismay, however, Karen told them that she was planning to stay at the Sheraton Hotel.

Before Karen left for Boston, she wasn't sure if these people were actually going to be her long lost family. So, as a precautionary measure, she booked a room at a hotel. On the way to the house, Karen told the family about Regina, the life she had led, how she was an attorney, and that Regina was a very good mother to her. But every time she referred to Regina as her mother, Mrs. Johnson got offended. Karen explained to them that she had no memory of what happened to her, but she was always suspicious of Regina. She also told them that Regina was a good person, and she didn't want to get her in trouble with the law. When the limo pulled up in front of the Johnson home, Karen started to remember running up and down the stairs in front of her house when she was younger. Mrs. Johnson didn't even have to lead her to her room, because she remembered exactly where it was. Karen was starting to regain her memory and the first thing that came back to her was how mean her dad was. She was almost frightened by him all of a sudden, and Mr. Johnson could sense it.

The Johnsons knew they had found their daughter, but Karen had also started a new life back in California. Her job, home, and everything she had known for the last fifteen years or so was in California. She would have to get to know her biological family all over again, and she wanted to know why Mr. Johnson frightened her. The whole family had to explain to her that her daddy was a changed man, and that he had come a long way to be a better father to Eddy and a husband to his wife. Karen was happy with the news, and she made plans to spend a week in Boston with her family. She was able to cancel her reservation at the Sheraton, and stayed in her old room at the Johnson house.

That week Karen discovered herself all over again. The family explained the tragedy with Mike, and how all this mess came about. Karen herself started to recall the events that led up to her disappearance. She also told her parents that she was lucky to have been found by Regina because she provided her with the best care and the best that life had to offer. She wanted her family to meet Regina. She told them that if they didn't mind, she would like to keep the name Sonya Watson. It would be too much trouble to change her name back to Karen because all of her professional achievements were attained in that name, and everyone in her professional life knew her as Sonya Watson. She still wanted her family to keep calling her Karen.

Even though it took a lot of work for Karen to finally find her family, the reality was that if Jimmy was not a star athlete with unlimited means, it would have been impossible. Unlike the Natalee Holloways of the world, Karen was a little black girl who went missing and the country didn't give a damn. Natalee Holloway went missing in Aruba and the whole world knew about it a few hours later, all because she had no melanin on her skin. Even in Aruba, a heavily populated black country, the black man was the first person to be under suspicion when she disappeared. Jimmy knew that young white boys all over the world know that they can always pull a fast one on the authorities everywhere by blaming the black man for violent acts. Society continues to perpetuate those sentiments by acting hastily to get these black men locked up.

It was easy for the Johnson family and Karen to keep their discovery from the media. The case had been closed and nobody except the family had been relentless enough in their search to find her. "So many young black girls have gone missing, and the police and the media hardly pay any attention to it. It seems almost as if these people's lives do not matter as much. The Jon Benet Ramseys, the Natalee Holloways and the Staci Petersons are the only types of women that the world seem to care about. Even when witnesses come forward with information about missing, little, black girls they are ignored. The young black girl who was found decapitated in Florida could've been saved if the police acted on the information from a witness. The struggle goes on for equality in a different way. Most people in the hood have no idea that there is still a struggle going on and a fight to be fought," Jimmy told the family.

Though Karen was happy to be reunited with her family, she had decided to go back to Los Angeles to stay because it had become her home and she did not want to leave the place that she had grown to love. Karen knew that a part of her truly loved Regina for all that she had done for her, and she didn't want to abandon her. She promised to keep in touch with her family and visit them as often as possible. Karen was happy to finally rediscover her true roots, but she was grateful for the life that she led under the care of Regina. Saying goodbye to her family on the last day of her visit wasn't easy. It was especially hard when her brother, Eddy, got teary eyed from the joy of finally seeing his sister again. Eddie was also happy that she was staying in California, because he now had someone and a new place to visit.

The Set-up

Despite the fact that Jimmy had helped reunite Karen with the family, his problem still hadn't gone away. Pastor Jacobs had devised a plan to deal with Jean, and his plan required him to spend endless amounts of time following Jean around. He knew that old habits were hard to break. Jean could not really give up prostitution and all the other bad habits like being a shoplifter and booster as well as a heroin addict. Pastor Jacobs started following Jean around with a hidden camera and it was easy for him to do, because she had no idea who he was. Jimmy had pointed Jean out to Pastor Jacobs one day while Pastor Jacobs purposely drove by the shelter.

Instead of getting up and go out to look for work everyday as required by the shelter, Jean had other plans. But Pastor Jacobs also had plans of his own. He invested almost a thousand dollars in a small camera that he was able to attach to his cap. Watching all those undercover stories on Dateline and other investigative shows on television taught Pastor Jacobs a thing or two about surveillance. He followed Jean around for most of the day and captured every criminal act she committed on camera. He saved the footage for the day when he would use it to get rid of her permanently.

Unaware that she was being watched, Jean was committing grand theft, shooting drugs, prostitution, and all kinds of other petty crime on the streets. The footage that Pastor Jacobs captured would have been great for an undercover story about Jean's life of crime. There were also other victims captured in this footage, and most of them happened to be very well known fathers and husbands getting blowjobs from Jean in the back of different cars. It was the type of footage that Jean and her clients did not want to end up in the hands of the media or the police. Pastor Jacobs had every intention on getting the footage to the police and media. Being from the streets had its advantages, and Pastor Jacobs was a force to be reckoned with. His son was the most important person in his life, and he was willing to go to great lengths to protect him.

After gathering enough evidence for about a week to ensure Jean's permanent departure from Boston, Pastor Jacobs called Jimmy to set up a meeting with Jean for the initial payment. The meeting was to take place at a motel in Boston, and Jimmy was supposed to bring close to ten thousand dollars to keep .Jean from going to the police with her story. Jean was very excited when she received the call from Jimmy, and was glad that her plan to blackmail him was finally coming to fruition. After the meeting was scheduled, they both hung up. Pastor Jacobs told Jimmy that he had everything under control and the matter would be taken care of. There was a sigh of relief from Jimmy as he crossed his fingers.

While Pastor Jacobs and Jimmy were planning their moves, Jean was making plans of her own. Jean was not as stupid as Jimmy and Pastor Jacobs thought. She wanted to protect herself in case things didn't go accordingly. She was also from the streets, and she had learned a thing or two while she was on the streets as well. The meeting with Jimmy was taking place a week later, and Jean wanted to make sure that she captured everything from that meeting on camera. She rented a room at the far end of the motel, and she invested in a few equipments of her own. Jean had set up hidden cameras all over the room.

She made sure that Jimmy's face would show in every position when they would discuss their arrangements.

Reaching Out to a Friend

While the Johnson family was going through their ordeal in Boston, the missing piece to their family puzzle was desperately trying to reconnect with her children. After Candy moved to Phoenix and left Katrina back in Boston in the jungle to fend for herself, she had learned through the grapevine that Tony, her pimp, was killed on the streets. She wondered how Katrina was surviving on her own. Candy had made a special trip to Boston to seek out Katrina. Unfortunately, she had learned that Katrina was incarcerated at Framingham State Prison.

Since Candy left the streets and moved to Phoenix, she had changed her life completely. She opened a center for runaway teens. With her past experience, she wanted to help keep kids off the streets. She was able to hire a grant writer to write a proposal for her, and she got the local as well as the federal government to fund her program. Candy's proposal was passionate and the lady she hired to write the grant believed in her cause. She wanted to help young teens transform their lives, and the only way she could do that was if she started her own program. The city of Phoenix also welcomed her efforts to help keep runaway teens off the streets. Her program has been a success since its inception.

Candy, however, could never get a young girl named Katrina that she left behind in Boston out of her mind. She was now in a position where she could help Katrina. She decided to take a trip to Framingham to visit with Katrina at the prison. After visiting with Katrina during her visit in Boston, they decided to continue to communicate with each other through letters and the occasional collect calls that Katrina would charge to

Candy's home phone. It was a relationship that Katrina really needed because the staff at the prison was worried that she was becoming suicidal. Candy's letters gave her strength and Katrina started coming out of her depressed funk.

Candy sent money to the prison for Katrina's commissary, and she also sent books that helped keep up her spirit while she was in jail. Candy knew that Katrina's children were a sensitive subject to her, so she avoided talking about her children. It would only have demoralized Katrina's progress. The two of them were like sisters. In no time, Candy was coming to the prison to visit Katrina on a monthly basis. She told Katrina about the Teen Center she opened back in Phoenix, and that she had a job waiting for her when she got out of prison. Candy also felt that Katrina's experience in jail would be a great asset for her program because the participants would hear of her experiences firsthand. Katrina had gone through things that many of these young women could never imagine, and Candy wanted to be proactive with her participants by having a staff that lived through it all talk to them.

Candy's friendship kept Katrina sane while she was in jail, and Katrina's spirit gave Candy hope for her program. She knew that Katrina's pains were going to make a great difference in these kids' lives, and she wanted to encourage Katrina positively while she was in Jail. Candy gave her hope and strength, and Katrina taught her determination.

Establishing Her Position

When Katrina first got to the prison she had to establish her position there. She could either be a weak link or a leader. She chose to be a leader. Many of the women were trying to test her fighting skills, and Katrina was not shy about whipping an ass or two. In no time, she was known as one of the most feared women in that jail and nobody wanted to mess with her. Katrina had gotten into scuffles with some of the toughest women in that jail, and she came out victorious most of the time. After a while, people started going to Katrina for favors or they would ask her permission before they acted on anything. Katrina surrounded herself with a group of young women that were tough enough that they didn't need actions. Their words were loud enough. They taught each other how to box and they lifted weights to get strong and their clique was formidable.

There was one girl in particular that Katrina took under her wing when she first came to the prison, and she soon became known as young Star at the prison. No one at the prison knew Katrina's real name, so everybody referred to her as Star. This being the name she used whenever she was arrested. After a few of years of mentoring young Star in the prison, it was time to pass the baton to her as the next leader in the prison. Katrina was confident that young Star was strong enough to hold her grounds when she decided that she wanted to transfer to Arizona to be closer to Candy. Katrina asked the prison officials if she could finish the terms of her sentence in Arizona where Candy lived. Young Star was transferred to Katrina's cell and she took over Katrina's leadership role as Katrina was granted a transfer.

Young Star, however, was not as strong as Katrina thought. She was not ready to assume the leadership position that Katrina had created for her. Soon after Katrina left, it was a total disaster at the prison. Young Star didn't know how to keep the girls in Katrina's old crew in check and everybody started to turn against her. She woke up everyday fighting someone to prove herself. After a while, she got tired of fighting. As feisty as young Star was, she didn't want to go on fighting everyday of her life for the remainder of her forty-year sentence for double murder. She wasn't as strong as initially perceived, and her weakness was starting to show. Young Star decided that she didn't want to deal with all the hassles that were going on with the women at the prison anymore. She got tired of fighting for her life and a role she didn't know how to handle.

Young Star decided to end it all by tying the body of her uniform shirt around the bars on her cell. She then wrapped the arms of the shirt around her neck and hung herself. It was a shirt that Katrina had left for young Star with her prison number on it. It was also a gift that young Star treasured from her mentor. Her lifeless body was discovered the next day by one of the prison guards. On the record, she was buried as Star Bright, because the prison officials failed to document that Star Bright AKA Katrina had been transferred to a prison in Arizona to finish out her sentence.

A Second Chance

In Arizona, Katrina thrived at the prison. She decided to take a different approach to prison life when she arrived in Arizona. Her reputation as a tough woman and a fighter back in Framingham followed her to Arizona. The inmates there knew better than to mess with her. Katrina also used her reputation to foster change in the prison system in Arizona. Of course, she had to make an example of the baddest and toughest woman at the prison when she first arrived to confirm her reputation, but after that it was smooth sailing. She had proven herself to her fellow inmates. The only thing she realized she could do with the fear that she instilled in them was to make them see things in a positive light.

Katrina became a model prisoner in no time and whenever there was trouble with the inmates, the guards sought her help to bring about peace. Katrina was on a first name basis with the warden, and she did more to assist them than any prisoner who had been at that prison in previous years. She also received a lot of privileges that other inmates didn't have. Candy visited with Katrina twice a week. Katrina was even able to convince the warden to allow Candy to bring a group of girls from the program to see what it was really like behind bars.

Katrina also ran a substance abuse group while in prison. She helped the younger inmates deal with their addiction while discussing her own past and addiction on the streets. Katrina never let anyone in on her private life, though. Nobody at the prison knew that she had children, and she made sure she didn't mention her family even during emotional moments in group with the other women. Katrina was a role model for many of the inmates at the prison. She inspired many of them to change their lives while in prison, and to stay positive after they were released back to society.

After serving almost half of the remaining sentence, Katrina was up for parole. She went before the parole board. With the help of the staff at the prison, she was granted parole and released from prison after serving thirteen years. The day before Katrina was released the guards and the inmates threw her a going-away party. Everyone was teary- eyed, because they knew that no one at that jail deserved their freedom more than Katrina. They also knew that they were losing a friend and a great person. Katrina left the prison with tears of joy as well as tears of loss, because she knew that she was going to miss her friends very soon. But freedom was a lot better.

Free At Last

When Katrina walked outside those prison gates, she also left behind the name Star Bright. She decided to go back to using her real name Katrina Johnson. After making her way outside the prison gates, she found Candy waiting in her BMW, X5 SUV. The first item on the menu was to get Katrina home into some better clothes and then take her shopping for a new wardrobe. Katrina could not believe that she was out of prison, and was about to face the world all over again. Candy had mentioned to her that Jimmy had become a professional basketball player and a good humanitarian and that her daughter Nina was a police officer. While visiting Boston, Candy went back to the old neighborhood to make sure that Katrina's children were okay. Katrina's mind was at ease knowing that her children had made it in this cruel world, but she wasn't ready to face them just yet. She felt that she had so much to prove to them for letting them down, but she didn't know where to begin.

Katrina had been denied a bath for the last thirteen years, and one of the things she was most looking forward to was a simple soothing bubble bath. Candy was so happy to see her friend out of prison, she didn't even argue Katrina's request. She drove straight to her four-bedroom home in suburban Phoenix to allow Katrina the luxury of a bath. Katrina's mouth almost hit the floor as Candy drove through her exclusive neighborhood with posh homes and well manicured lawns lining the streets. She couldn't believe that her friend had come so far. Candy had taken her fifty thousand dollars and invested it wisely.

When she first got to Phoenix, she enrolled in an adult education degree program offered at University of

Phoenix. She pursued a Bachelor's Degree in Counseling while she worked as a receptionist at a counseling center during the day. Candy completed her degree in two and a half years and then went on to pursue her PhD in Psychology. She kept all her personal achievements from Katrina when she was in jail because she did not want Katrina to think that she expected her to live up to those expectations.

Candy didn't waste too much time after she left Tony. She wanted to change her life and she knew that the only way she could do that was to go back to school and earn a degree. Someone with her background would have had too much of a hard time making it in the world. Candy had also regained custody of her daughter who was now an adult working as the Executive Assistant Director at her mother's center. Katrina was in awe of Candy and she knew that she couldn't ask for a better friend. Candy was the kind of friend who only used positive reinforcements with Katrina, and she never once made Katrina feel like she was above her because she was a doctor.

Candy pressed the automatic garage door opener in her two car garage as she pulled in the driveway, and Katrina noticed the brand new CLK 320, Mercedes in the garage. Candy handed a set of keys to Katrina for the Benz as well as keys to the house so she could come and go as she pleased. Katrina didn't know what to say to Candy, but she was even more shocked after she entered the house. The door from the garage led them right to the sit-in style kitchen where Katrina saw the most beautiful hardwood floors, stainless steel kitchen appliances, and furniture that money could buy.

Katrina was even more shocked when she raised her head
to the twelve-foot vaulted ceilings from the kitchen to the
formal dining room. The chandelier hanging from the
ceiling in the dining room looked like something a person
would find in the home of a movie star. Candy had come
a long way, and she didn't spare any luxury in that house.

All the bedrooms in the house were fully furnished with
top-notch furniture from some of the hottest, high-end
designers in the business. In the back yard, there was an
Olympic size swimming pool, as well as a Jacuzzi that
was big enough to accommodate a whole football team.
Candy led Katrina to the guest bedroom, located on the
first floor of the house. There was a full bathroom and
plenty of room to help her adjust from a ten-by-ten jail
cell to a life of luxury. Life as Katrina knew it was about
to change and change for the better. The first thing she did
when she entered the room was to fall back on the plush
bed covered with satin sheets. She took off all her clothes
and headed to the bathroom. Katrina took one of the
longest baths that day as she savored every minute of her
newfound freedom.

Later that night, Candy cooked Katrina the best meal that
she had ever had. Candy had learned to become a great
cook after she regained custody of her daughter. As a
mother, she couldn't rely on McDonald's and other
restaurants to keep her daughter healthy. She might have
been a career woman, but she was also a mother and a
mother who cared deeply for her daughter. Having been
neglected by her own parents, Candy made sure that she
gave her daughter the attention that she needed. As a
result, her daughter also became a doctor. Candy's new
task, however, was to help ease Katrina's assimilation
back into society.

Adjusting to Her New life

Candy knew that life behind bars was rough on Katrina and she wanted to help make the transition as smooth as possible. As a psychologist, she wanted to counsel Katrina, but there was a conflict of interest because Katrina was her friend. She knew that every little banging noise would send Katrina in a state of paranoia because of the slamming sound of the prison doors, so she kept her noise to a minimum during the first few months of Katrina's release. She also gave Katrina time to recuperate and decide which direction she wanted to take her life.

Of course, Candy had a job waiting for Katrina at the center, but she left it up to her to decide when she would be ready to work. Katrina's experience as a drug counselor was invaluable to Candy's program because many of the children who came to the center were victims of drug abuse as well. It took Katrina a few weeks to get acclimated, but she was ready to tackle the challenge. Katrina had an infectious personality, and when she started working at the center the girls gravitated towards her almost immediately. She was running her own groups in no time, and the young girls could not wait to hear about her hard life in jail and on the streets. As entertaining as Katrina's life sounded to them, she warned them to take her stories seriously because she didn't want any of them to fall victim to the circumstances she did. Katrina tried as blatantly as she could to tell the young girls in the program about her harsh life behind bars and on the streets. Unlike most people from the ghetto who served time, Katrina didn't want to glorify prison life and made it a point to tell these young girls about the barriers that a prison record could create.

Everyone at the center loved Katrina, and Candy could depend on her to make sure things were running smoothly when she had to go away on conferences. Candy's daughter had become a younger sister to Katrina, and they even hung out sometimes. Katrina stayed away from all the bad elements that sent her to jail, and Candy made sure that she received counseling from one of her colleagues twice a week. Everything in Katrina's life was finally coming together, and she had Candy to thank for her successful transition.

After living with Candy for close to a year, Katrina was ready to be on her own. She knew that Candy had made adjustments in her own life to accommodate her while living with her. She didn't want to be a burden any longer. When she told Candy that she was ready to get her own place, Candy only asked where she wanted to live. They went apartment hunting together, and with the help of Candy and her daughter, Katrina secured a nice apartment in a middle-class neighborhood on the outskirts of Phoenix. She continued to work for Candy and she earned a healthy salary. Katrina, Candy, and her daughter would sometimes hang out together. They would have a ball laughing at the men who tried to pick them up when they were out. The ladies were all appealing and attractive in their own right and they flaunted what they had every chance they got. Katrina managed to regain her beauty after sobering up. She was able to get her teeth replaced because Candy knew a great dentist who did magical work with veneers.

Family's Never Lost

Despite all the positive changes in Katrina's life and all the progress that she had made, one thing remained constant; the inability to face her children. The psychologist worked with Katrina on the issues relevant to her children, but she was always too ashamed to muster the courage to face them. She had written letters to them while she was in prison, but she never got a response from them. Actually, the letters never made it to Jimmy and Nina, because they had moved from the house by the time she started writing to them.

Candy didn't want to pressure Katrina about her kids every time they hung out, but she urged her to try to reconcile with them. It was at least worth a try. She even offered to fly to Boston with Katrina to face her children. Katrina did not know where to begin, and she did not know where to find her kids. Candy put those worries to rest very quickly when she got on her computer and did a search on Nina and found out that she lived in Hyde Park with her husband. Katrina had no idea that her children had reconnected with her parents, so Candy also looked up her parents on the Internet. She found out that they still lived in the same house where Katrina grew up. Candy told her it was still worth a try to reach out to her parents, and burying old hatchets was very important to new beginnings. Candy also suggested that Katrina go back to her old neighborhood to see what people had to say about Jimmy and Nina, so she could have a better idea on how to approach them. "People in the hood are always honest about certain things. They always seem to know what is going on in people's lives even after they are long gone from the neighborhood." Candy told Katrina.

The decision to face her children was something that Katrina really struggled with, and the feeling of failure continued to linger within. Katrina had seen Jimmy grow up to be a very handsome man only on television, but she never had a chance to see Nina. She wondered if her little girl had grown up to be a lady. There was so much on Katrina's mind, she decided the best thing to do was to face the situation. She booked a flight to Boston to go see her children alone.

A Jungle No More

Katrina landed in Boston a changed woman. She rented a car at the airport and headed straight to her old neighborhood. Katrina didn't even bother to go to her hotel downtown to check in. She was eager to see all the old familiar faces in her neighborhood. Unfortunately, there were no more familiar faces left. The neighborhood had changed drastically and all the bad memories had been erased. The derelict tenements had been refurbished to look brand new again. The street was newly paved and lined up with trees. The front yards of the homes were filled with beautiful gardens and well-manicured lawns. Even the old house where Katrina rented her first apartment looked different. Since Nina bought it, she added new vinyl siding, windows, and a new front porch to compliment the totally renovated interior.

Katrina was back to square one. There was no one that she could reconnect with or ask questions. All her old friends had been swept off that street to make room for the re-gentrified group of yuppies and buppies who found their way back to the city due to the convenient commute to the center of town. She didn't even know that her daughter had bought the house where she once lived. Katrina felt like she was in a strange place. Her only hope now was the address that she had for Nina in Hyde Park. There was no one on Kentworth Street to help her prepare for the meeting with her daughter. It was then or never; Katrina had come too far to turn back. She was about to do the hardest thing ever in her life as a mother, which was facing the children that she had neglected years ago.

The Jungle that Katrina left behind had been transformed to a beautiful garden. It was a matter of time before

Katrina got word that a new jungle had been created about thirty miles south of Boston in Brockton. Most of the crack heads that were forced out of the hood found their way to an old factory city that had lost its luster when the factories were shut down. The great white hope Rocky Marciano had made Brockton famous when he became the only undefeated boxer to retire with his heavyweight belt featuring a record of 49-0. Katrina knew that Larry Holmes broke that record when he fought Leon Spinks, but the white world was not ready to give up Marciano's record to a black man. Not to mention the countless times that Rocky Marciano himself lost to other great black boxers who were cheated because the white judges were not fair to them. Katrina knew this because she was a boxing fan and she used to watch the fights with her dad as a little girl. It was the only thing that they ever did together.

Katrina also knew that White people have never been fair to black folks since they visited the African continent. They were not fair to her and her children. They were not fair to the people on Kentworth Street. They were not fair to the people in Africa whose resources they have stolen since the beginning of time. They were not fair to the Indians whose land they stole while annihilating most of the population. They were not fair to the Mexicans whose land they stole in the West and now try to ridicule them by tagging them with the label "illegal immigrants." They are not fair to the Haitian people who helped them fight off the French for the great state of Louisiana and the great battle in Savannah, Georgia. They are not fair for supplying the hood with crack and illegal guns. They are not fair for allowing the devastating disease known as AIDS to massacre almost half of Africa, India, and Asia. They are not fair for trying to become dictators to the rest of the world and Katrina knew this now because she spent a lot of her time reading in jail reading history books as well.

Katrina was now better equipped to understand that White people pretty much want to control the world and to some extent they do. They originated from Europe, but somehow they managed to own the majority of land and wealth in some of the richest parts of the world. They managed to own all the gold and diamond mines in Africa, they control parts of Asia, they took America from the Indians and the Mexicans, and now they are trying to conquer the only part of the world where they have never been able to stake claim, the Middle East. So Katrina knew that the hood was only a dot on the map and it was at their disposal for the taken whenever they chose. She also noticed how quickly the ghetto can be cleaned up when White folks want to make it their home again. In the grand scheme of things, these people had also contributed indirectly to her harsh life on the street.

"What happens locally in our neighborhoods has taken place globally since the beginning of time. Whatever is convenient for rich white people can easily become an inconvenience not just black people but poor people all over the world," Katrina thought to herself. Katrina's old neighborhood was part of the new convenience and the old crack heads were made to be inconvenient somewhere else. Thus, Katrina had lost all her connections to her old neighborhood.

Facing the Music

True to form, Katrina was a survivor and not a quitter. She hopped back in her car and drove straight to Nina's house in Hyde Park. On the way to the house, Katrina's emotions of guilt overcame her, and she started to break down and cry in the car. As a mother, she had failed her kids, and it was the one thing that she couldn't go back and change. Moving forward was one thing, but looking your little girl in the eyes and trying to explain to her that drugs and prostitution were more important than being a mother was another thing all together. The survival argument would not work because Nina had to survive herself and she didn't turn to prostitution. Katrina wanted to face the music, but she didn't know what tune to expect.

She couldn't make up her mind about what she wanted to say, and she drew a blank every time she was trying to rehearse something from memory. Everything was failing Katrina, but she didn't want to fail her children again. She had no idea about the agony the children went through when they thought she was dead. Katrina only believed that her children turned their backs on her while she was locked up, but the children were living with the pain of her death for years. Katrina figured that only two things could happen as she pulled up in front of the house; Nina could reject or accept her. She knew that forgiveness would take time, but acceptance would open the door for her to earn Nina's forgiveness.

Katrina was all smiles as she pulled up in front of the big Victorian house. She double-checked the numbers of the address on the piece of paper in her purse to make sure it was correct. From the look of the house alone, Katrina knew that her daughter had made it out the slums of Boston. She looked in the mirror to make sure that her hair and make-up were right before stepping out of the rental car. Walking up the ten steps to Nina's front door seemed like eternity. Katrina was nervous and happy at the same time. Before ringing the door bell, she took notice of the Mercedes Benz parked in the driveway near the garage, and she was all smiles. "Her daughter had indeed made it out of the slums," she thought. She fixed her clothes once more as she rang the doorbell. It took a little while for Nina to come to the door because she was trying to feed her youngest child. Meanwhile Katrina contemplated leaving, because it was taking too long for someone to answer the door.

She began to think she was making a mistake and as she turned to walk back down towards her car, a voice called out, "Can I help you?" Katrina took a deep breath before she turned around to face her daughter. As Katrina turned around and said, "I'm looking for Nina?!" Nina ran towards her and exclaimed, "Mom!" She was elated to see her mother as she reached her and gave her an eternal embrace. The butterflies in Katrina's stomach, before she saw her daughter, were replaced by joy and happiness. The two women hugged until tears started flowing like rainfall dropping out of the sky during hurricane season in Florida.

Nina couldn't believe her eyes. "How is it possible that you're still alive?" she asked her mother. "It's a long story and I will tell you all about it as soon as I'm able to stop rejoicing in this moment," Katrina answered. She invited Katrina inside as she made her way back to her daughter in the kitchen. She introduced Katrina to her children. She started telling her about her husband, children, and grandparents like two friends who hadn't seen each other in years and needed to catch up in life. Nina made Katrina feel so welcomed that the guilt that Katrina initially felt started to resurface. She realized that her kids had no idea that she was alive and again she had failed to reach out to them to make sure that they knew where she was. Nina hadn't even brought up the fact that the prison officials had categorized her as "dead." The joy in Nina's face completely took away Katrina's pain and suffering for all the time she didn't see her children. She went over and hugged Nina once more before the tears started flowing again. She sat there and watched how beautiful and gorgeous her daughter had turned out to be. She also took notice of Nina's growing stomach with her third grandchild.

After feeding her daughter, little Katrina, Nina told her mother that she had named her daughter after her. After she learned from the prison officials that her mother had committed suicide, she wanted to keep her name alive. Nina explained to her mother that the prison officials had listed her as dead. Katrina had gotten news that young Star had committed suicide after she left the prison in Massachusetts, but she didn't know that the prison officials had mistakenly listed her as the person who died. She explained to Nina that it was mistake that the prison officials had made, but she made her own mistake by assuming that her children had turned their backs on her. They even started laughing at the fact that everyone cried for her at young Star's funeral.

Katrina was anxious to learn about Jimmy. She knew that he was a basketball star from watching him on television all the time, but she wanted to know how he dealt with the fact that he thought his mother was dead. Nina tried her best to explain to her mother that it was harder for Jimmy to cope with the loss at first, but he had forgiven her and was able to move on with his life. She also told Katrina that her presence was going to be the biggest surprise in Jimmy's life. "If there was one thing he could use right now that was some good news because he hadn't been in a good mood lately." Nina told her mother. She started telling Katrina about Jimmy's battle with kidney failure. Katrina told her she missed the whole thing, as it unfolded on television, because she couldn't bear to watch her child suffer.

There was so much that Katrina wanted to say to her daughter, but she simply sat back and relished in the moment as she watched her daughter and her grandchildren. There was really no word to describe the feeling that overcame Katrina on the day she saw her daughter. The word that would come closest to it would be "rapture." Katrina was caught up in the rapture and she didn't want the moment to end. She kissed and hugged her grandchildren many times over.

While Katrina may have been elated to see Nina, Nina couldn't wait to get on the phone to invite Jimmy over for a special visit. After dialing Jimmy's number, it took forever for him to pick up his cell phone. When he finally did, he was not in the best mood and Nina sensed it almost instantly. Jimmy was still trying to figure out a way to deal with his problems with Jean, and Pastor Jacobs hadn't come up with anything solid to make her go away completely yet. Nina told Jimmy that he needed to drop whatever he was doing and head to her house immediately. He asked, "Is it an emergency?" She told him "Yes!" He asked, "Are the kids all right?" She told him "Yes!" He then asked, "What's the emergency?" She informed him that she couldn't tell him on the phone, but he needed to bring his butt to her house right away. He told her that he would be right over then hung up the phone.

A Great Surprise

Jimmy hopped in his car instantly to go find out what was up with his sister. While driving over to her house he wondered what was so important that she wanted him to come over right away. He hoped that it was not something serious that needed his attention. Jimmy had his hand full with Jean, and he was looking for relief not more headaches. He was relying on Pastor Jacobs to make his problem go away, but Pastor Jacobs was not coming up with a solution that was quick enough for him. Jimmy did not want his life ruined in the media and he damn sure did not want someone to take advantage of something that he had worked hard for all his life. There was no point of beating himself up for something that he felt he had no control over. He crossed his fingers hoping that the situation would be resolved with the help of Pastor Jacobs.

Jimmy pulled up in front of Nina's house and noticed the burgundy, Ford Crown Victoria parked outside. The first thing that ran through his mind after seeing the car parked in front of the house was that Jean had called the police to scare him into paying her. It was a well-known fact in Boston that all the undercover cops drove the big Ford, Crown Victoria. Jimmy hesitated, at first, because he thought he was about to get caught and the police were using his family to get to him. He thought about running, then he realized that there was nowhere in the world he could go without being recognized. A well-known basketball player, there was no place to hide.

Jimmy sat in the car and sweat for a little while before deciding to face his fate. As much as he anticipated a big hoopla with the Boston Police Department, he was about to dance to a whole different beat; a beat that would bring a bittersweet feeling. After ringing the doorbell a couple of times, Jimmy braced himself for the handcuffs that he expected the cops to slap around his wrists. He stood there sweating for about thirty seconds before Nina came to the door. Jimmy realized that there was nothing wrong from the big smile his sister was wearing on her face. He was relieved to see that she was happy, but he still wondered why.

As the two of them stepped back into the living room, Nina told Jimmy that she had a pleasant surprise for him, and it was something that he would have never expected. When Jimmy stepped into the living room, he recognized his mother right away. He ran towards her and gave her a bear hug, lifting her up from the floor leaving her feet suspended. She was begging for Jimmy to put her down. Katrina had never expected her boy to develop into such a huge man, and she also didn't expect the reception she got from both of her children. Jimmy was elated that she was still alive, and for a moment he'd forgotten about all his problems.

Jimmy and Nina sat in the living room as Katrina tried to bring them up to date to what she had been doing since her release from jail. She told them about her best friend, Candy, who helped her get her life together while she was in jail as well as the poor decision she made to stay away from them. She told them that she had been sober for years, and that prostitution and drugs were in her past and she intended to keep it that way. Jimmy had the same questions as Nina about her supposed death, and she explained to him it was all a mistake by the prison the department. Also, she appreciated all his effort in making sure that Young Star received a proper burial, because she was also a great person who deserved the same treatment. Jimmy was so happy to see his mother he didn't know what to do with himself. He kept holding her in his arms and didn't want to let go.

She told them about her new life in Phoenix, and that she really enjoyed being out there making a difference in the lives of the young girls in her program. Katrina was grateful that her kids had forgiven her, and was looking forward to getting to know them and catching up with their lives. Nina and Jimmy felt that the best part was yet to come as they told their mother that they were able to reconnect with their grandparents and Pastor Jacobs. Katrina's reaction to the news was not at all positive. She blamed her parents for a long time for the way her life turned out, and she was not ready to forgive them for turning their backs on her.

It was hard for the kids to read Katrina's facial expression, but they were hoping that she would be happy with the news. Katrina had never mentioned her parents to her children in the past because she harbored ill feelings towards them. She never anticipated that a family reunion would take place between her children and her parents. She didn't even bother to ask them how her parents were doing. She did, however, ask who Pastor Jacobs was. When Jimmy told her that Leon, the hustler, had become a Pastor, the first words out of her mouth were "I guess he found a new hustle!"

The kids didn't want to condone the negative vibes they were getting from their mother about Pastor Jacobs and their grandparents. They had come a long way to bring the family back together, and they didn't want their mother to come in and destroy all the hard work that they had done. Katrina was just as guilty as her parents when she turned her back on them, and they made sure that they let her know it. She was the pot calling the kettle black, and the kids didn't want to hear anything negative from her about the people in their lives.

If Katrina wanted to be part of their lives, she would have to learn to forgive just like they did. There was no other way. As happy as Nina and Jimmy were to see that their mother was still alive, they were not willing to create a division in the family because of her. Forgiveness was something new to Katrina, and she had to learn from her children how to forgive and forget. The kids made no qualms about the fact that they were happy to see her and wanted her to be part of the family again, but they were not willing to take her side against their grandparents and Pastor Jacobs.

Nina and Jimmy tried as much as they could to explain to their mother how sorry their grandparents were for turning their backs on her. Even Pastor Jacobs was a new man who wished that he had never turned his back on her. While behind bars, Katrina thought about writing her parents to ask them to help care for her children, but she never followed through with it. She knew that she had no right to hold grudges because she would be just as bad as the people she was holding the grudge against. Katrina made a pact with her children that she would forgive her parents and Pastor Jacobs, because the most important thing to her was their happiness. She had failed them once; she didn't want to ruin it again the second time around.

Jimmy and Nina asked how long she was in Boston for and Katrina told them she was not sure, because she did not know how they were going to receive her. Extending her stay in Boston was only a matter of a phone call to Candy. She told them that she only brought clothes for a couple of days, however, Jimmy and Nina told her not to worry about clothes because they could always take her shopping. They asked her to stay for a couple of weeks, splitting her time between Jimmy and Nina's house. Katrina took out her cell phone to tell Candy the good news, and Candy had no problem with her extending her stay in Boston. She was more than happy to grant Katrina a two-week vacation.

After finalizing her plans with Nina and Jimmy, Katrina called the hotel to cancel her reservation. A dinner was planned at Jimmy's house in two days at six o'clock in the evening so that they could bring the whole family back together. Everybody was expected to be there to welcome Katrina back to her family. Nina told her kids not to say anything to their father about their grandmother coming to the house, and if they kept her secret she would take them to get their favorite ice cream the upcoming Sunday.

Getting Acquainted

Nina and Jimmy kept Katrina's presence a secret from their grandparents, Pastor Jacobs, Eddy, Karen, and Collin. Everyone was called and invited to Jimmy's house for a special dinner in a couple of days, and the time was rescheduled for eight o'clock in the evening in order to accommodate everyone's schedule. Jimmy even placed a call to his aunt Karen in California to ask her to come to Boston promptly due to an emergency. Karen did not even question Jimmy's motives as she called the airline to make reservations to come to Boston the following day.

The only person who knew about Katrina other than Jimmy and Nina was Lisa, and that was only because Jimmy brought her over to his house to stay with him for the first week. When Katrina first arrived at Jimmy's house, she couldn't believe her eyes. She thought she had seen the nicest house that she would ever see back in Phoenix when Candy took her home. Jimmy's house was ten times bigger and twenty times more beautiful. Candy was doing well, but she didn't have millionaire money like Jimmy did.

Getting accustomed to seeing high priced homes and luxuries that Katrina never before knew existed was going to be a huge adjustment for her. It was a big one hundred eighty degree change for her. Jimmy's house was lavish and everything in the home was grand. His money was well spent by Lisa when she decided to decorate the place herself. The spiral staircase overlooking the foyer at the entrance of the house is reminiscent of a castle from an old kingdom. The twelve-foot ceilings added to the Victorian flair and the grandiose stature of the house.

Katrina requested a tour of the house and Jimmy obliged.
Jimmy had the house completely renovated, and added a
gym fully equipped with every kind of exercise
equipment that he could find. He had free weights as well
as universal weights and a regulation size indoor
basketball court. He wanted to start with the gym because
that was where he spent most of his time. By the time he
made his way back to the family room, he asked Lisa to
take over the tour while he lounged on the couch.
Katrina's mouth remained open throughout the tour, and
she couldn't believe how far her son had come. She was
just as impressed with Lisa. She noticed that Lisa was
well mannered, easy going, caring, and sincere. They
instantly bonded. Lisa had grown up to be a beautiful
woman and her assets had grown in all the right places.
The little shy girl that Jimmy met in high school was no
longer. She had blossomed to a gorgeous woman with a
great sense of style.

As they were going around the house, Katrina and Lisa
engaged in a conversation that involved Jimmy. She
wanted to know if her son was happy and if they were
planning on having children any time soon. Lisa and
Jimmy had been trying to get pregnant, but since the re-
emergence of Jean, Jimmy's mind had been elsewhere.
Lisa knew her husband, and she figured in due time he
would come around and they would start having great sex
once again. Katrina acted more like a best friend with
Lisa, and she loved it. When they were done with the tour,
Katrina was impressed and hungry. Lisa offered to cook
dinner as her husband was hungry, too.

Katrina went back to the living room to catch up with her
son while Lisa went into the kitchen to whip up
thing to eat. Katrina was sitting in the family room

staring at Jimmy as if she could not believe her eyes. He was actually sitting in front of her with all his wealth and success! He had grown to a mature and handsome man, but she could tell that something was on his mind. Even though she had been away from him for a long time, she still had motherly instincts. Her motherly instincts told her that something was bothering her son.

She asked 'do you have something on your mind that you want to talk about, son? I may have been away from you for a long time, but I can still sense when something is bothering you, you know?" He told her that it was nothing that he couldn't handle on his own. She wanted to know what it was, and she told him that he never knew what solution she could come up with as a mother unless he told her his problem. Katrina was walking a thin line with Jimmy, because Jimmy got involved in this mess to begin with because of her. If he had not confronted his mother's john, he wouldn't have been implicated in a murder. The more she tried to get Jimmy to talk, the more enraged he became. After pestering him for a while, he blurted out to her, "it's your fault that my life may be ruined by this woman." Katrina had no idea what Jimmy was talking about. The television was loud enough to drown out the sound of their conversation away from Lisa.

Jimmy decided to tell his mother about Jean and the murder of Patrick Ferry, and how it was now coming back to haunt him. After hearing Jimmy's story, Katrina felt that if she ever wanted to get in her son's good graces again, she had better come up with a solution to help him get rid of Jean. Jimmy told his mother that he never involved his wife in the situation, because he didn't want to worry her. He had intended to keep it that way.

Mom to the Rescue

Being an ex-con and a former street prostitute was no deterrent for Katrina after she heard Jimmy's story. She simply asked him for Jean's name and address. After eating the best spaghetti and meat sauce dish ever cooked by Lisa, Katrina grabbed her car keys and headed straight to the Kind Street Inn where Jean was staying. She told Jimmy she was going to visit an old friend and she would be back later that night. Her experience in jail had toughened Katrina up to the point where she was fearless, and physical confrontation was the least of her worries.

Armed with a gray wig, bifocal glasses, and a cane that she purchased from a joke store before her visit with Jean, Katrina was determined to help Jimmy out of his situation. She tried as much as she could to disguise herself by wrapping a silk scarf around her head on top of the wig, and she changed her voice to that of an old, frail woman. Katrina went to the front desk and asked for Jean Murray. She was told that Jean had not reported back to the shelter, but she was due back in less than a half hour in order to beat the shelter's curfew. Katrina decided to wait for Jean down the block in her car for forty-five minutes.

Katrina moved her car a few blocks down the street and she started losing her patience. After noticing this woman walking into the shelter, she went back to the front desk and once again asked if Jean came back. This time the lady at the front desk pointed Jean out to her as Jean was making her way through the lobby. The lady called for Jean to come back to meet with Katrina. When Jean ‑‑‑‑‑ around, Katrina told the receptionist "Never mind! not her." Katrina was able to take a good look at

Jean, and made sure she remembered her face. Katrina was also from the old school, she knew from Jean's attire that she hadn't fully given up prostitution. She would find a way to sneak out of the shelter later that evening to go work the streets. After all, Jimmy's big checks hadn't started rolling in yet.

She went outside and waited patiently in her car for Jean to reappear. As expected, Jean snuck out through the back door, and Katrina met her in the back alley. She approached Jean and asked her, "Do you know Jimmy?" Jean responded, "What business is it of yours?" Katrina rebutted, "If you know what's good for you, you'd leave him alone and not ever try to get in touch with him again." Jean sarcastically answered, "What you gonna do, beat my ass, grandma?" Katrina told, "Leave Jimmy alone and everything will be all right. If you come within a hundred feet of Jimmy or his home, you will have me to deal with!" Jean could only laugh after she heard Katrina's statement, and then told Katrina that if Jimmy didn't pay up she'd make sure that his life was ruined.

At this point, Jean was starting to wear out Katrina's patience. The tough ex-con was about to emerge once more. Katrina tried to grab Jean's arm in an intimidating way to show her that she was serious. Before she could grab a hold of Jean's hands, Jean pulled out a knife that she usually carried for protection. She extended the blade and cut Katrina across the hand as she was reaching out to grab her. Katrina backed up to watch the blood spill out of her hand, and before Jean could flinch she hit Jean over the head with the cane in her right hand. Jean fell to the ground. The cane slipped out of Katrina's hand as she hit Jean again. Jean charged at Katrina flinging the knife at her, trying to stab her with it.

She had pushed Katrina all the way back against the wall away from the cane, and there was nowhere for Katrina to go. With one last attempt to stab Katrina in the heart, Jean swung the knife as hard as she could, but Katrina ducked and was stabbed on the shoulder instead.

Jean tried jumping on her to finish her off, but Katrina was able to push Jean off of her. She noticed a piece of lead pipe lying on the ground. She dove to the ground and picked up the pipe, as Jean got back on top of her attempting to stab her again. Katrina was able to get her hand on the lead pipe, but not before Jean stabbed her twice on her right leg. She was able to kick Jean off of her with her left leg, and used the lead pipe as support to get up from the ground. They were now facing each other: Jean with a knife in hand and Katrina with a twenty-inch piece of lead pipe and a few stab wounds. Jean took a couple of swing at Katrina with the knife and missed. Reverting to her fighting skills back in prison, Katrina was able to set Jean up with a left hook, and as Jean got closer to her she hit her across the head with the pipe. Jean was knocked out.

Katrina became angry as she got on top of Jean, and continued to beat the crap out of her using the lead pipe. By the time she was able to regain her composure, Jean's lifeless body lay on the ground. Katrina picked up the lead pipe, her cane, and the knife from Jean's hand and hobbled off to her car. Unfortunately, there was an eyewitness who watched the whole thing unfold from her window in the back alley. When Katrina got to her car around the corner, she took off the gray wig and placed it in a bag along with the knife and lead pipe. She then locked the bag in her trunk with the cane. She was profusely bleeding from her wounds, but the hospital was the last place she wanted to go.

The meeting between Jean and Jimmy in the motel room would never take place, and she would never get the money that she anticipated would change her life forever. Jean's demise was Jimmy's fortune, just like his demise would have been hers. As a mother, Katrina seemed to have been able to reconnect with her family just in the nick of time. But now, she needed to make sure that the sound of steel bars and gates would not be her fate once again.

United Once More

Katrina called Jimmy at his home to ask for Pastor Jacobs' number. Jimmy had mentioned to her that Pastor Jacobs was the only other person who knew about Jean and he was the only one helping him. Jimmy wanted to know why Katrina needed Pastor Jacob's number, and she told him she just wanted to call and thank him for watching after him and Nina. After Katrina got off the phone with Jimmy, she immediately placed a call to Pastor Jacobs. Mrs. Jacobs picked up the phone and Katrina asked to speak with her husband. Pastor Jacobs had a surprised reaction to a female calling his home so late at night.

When he got on the phone, Katrina told him that she had an emergency and she needed his help because it had to do with Jimmy. Pastor Jacobs didn't believe that the caller was Katrina because as far he was concerned, she was dead. She told him that she couldn't go into details on the telephone, but he needed to meet her in the parking lot of Roxbury Community College as soon as possible if he didn't want to see Jimmy end up in jail. Katrina was familiar with the Roxbury Community College area because she had driven by it on her way to Nina's house earlier in the day. She noticed the changes right away, and she was pleased with the new buildings at the school and the total renovation of the area.

It was one thing for Pastor Jacobs to be suspicious of the caller, but it was an entirely different thing when it involved the livelihood of his only son. Katrina said things to him on the phone about their old time together, and he realized that only, she, would know such things as the place they used to have sex and which motel. Pastor

222

Jacobs jumped out of bed and told his wife that he had an emergency that he needed to tend to. He got up and threw on a sweat suit, and headed to Roxbury Community College to meet Katrina. On her way to Roxbury Community College, Katrina could see the barrage of police headlights and siren headed to the South End where she knew that she had just killed Jean. She was trying her best not to look suspicious as she carefully drove through traffic towards the college.

At one point on her way to the college parking lot, a police cruiser pulled up behind her with flashing lights and siren. She thought that they had caught up to her as she pulled over to the side of the road. But relief soon followed, as the police cruiser continued to head up the street pass Katrina. The police officer driving the cruiser was only trying to clear his path on his way to a dispatched call for another crime. All Katrina could think about at that moment was the fact that she had come back to Boston to get locked up again, and this time she knew it would be for good. This would be her second stint in jail for defending her children and there wasn't going to be any leniency on the part of the court.

After Katrina finally made it to the parking lot of the school, she impatiently waited for Pastor Jacobs to show up. She was bleeding profusely, and if he didn't get there soon she was going to pass out. She tried her best to apply pressure to her wounds, but there were too many wounds. After about ten minutes of fighting to stay awake, Pastor Jacobs pulled up in the parking lot in his Mercedes Benz. He noticed Katrina's rental car in the lot, and immediately ran towards it. He found her slouched in the front seat covered with blood. Pastor Jacobs never forgot her face, and he recognized Katrina instantly. He was asking her how she got stabbed, but she didn't have enough strength to answer. When he suggested taking her to the hospital, she shook her head saying, "No!"

Due to the nature of his work with children, Pastor Jacobs always kept a First-Aid Kit in the trunk of his car for emergencies. He was able to patch up Katrina's wounds and gave her a couple of aspirin to take away the pain. After Katrina regained her strength and consciousness, she tried to explain to Pastor Jacobs how she was attacked by Jean when she went to talk to her about Jimmy. After getting the full story from Katrina, Pastor Jacobs knew that taking her to the hospital was out of the question. She could not go on with just patches on her wounds. She needed to get stitches. While Katrina was in jail, she had to learn many things and stitching a wound happened to be one of them. Pastor Jacobs went to Walgreen's and bought Katrina a pack of dental floss and some needles. They went to his church and she sat in the basement stitching her wounds without so much as a scream from the pain inflicted by the needle. She had truly come a long way from the weaker Katrina that Pastor Jacobs met many years ago.

Pastor Jacobs wanted to know how Katrina was even still alive, but she was getting tired of telling the story over and over. She told him that he would have to wait until the family dinner at Jimmy's house in a couple of days to hear the story along with everybody else. "My presence was supposed to be a surprised but now you know!" she said.

She needed a plan to avoid going to jail and Pastor Jacobs was just the man to help keep her out of jail. Katrina also did not want Jimmy and Nina to know what she had done because she did not know how they would react. First, her car had to be cleaned of all the blood she had spilled. Pastor Jacobs took Katrina back to the parking lot to pick up the rental car. He had her follow him to his house so she could park the car in his garage. After securing the car in the garage, Pastor Jacobs took Katrina back to Jimmy's house. She tried her best to look presentable. Jimmy was too tired to notice how badly she really looked when he came to open the door. She was also wearing an overcoat that Pastor Jacobs took out of his wife's closet. She used it to hide her wounds from Jimmy. Before leaving, Katrina asked Pastor Jacobs not to say anything to her children about the incident. In fact, she wanted him to act like they had not seen each other yet at the dinner.

Katrina went to the guest bathroom and washed up before she went to sleep. She changed the gauze on her wounds and wore a long t-shirt to bed. She also took a couple of aspirins to ease her pain. It was an adventurous night for Katrina on her first day back to Boston. While she was lying in bed, she knew that Boston was not a place that she wanted to be because she constantly had a chain of bad luck following her. She knew that it was a matter of time before she perished for good in Boston. She vowed to stay in the house until the end of her visit in order to stay out of trouble.

Everyone's got something to hide

Katrina woke up the next morning to the smell of bacon, eggs, toasts, and freshly squeezed orange juice. She ran to the bathroom to brush her teeth. When she came out, she threw on a robe that Lisa left for her on the hook of her bedroom door. Jimmy and Lisa allowed her to get a good night sleep. Lisa decided to run to the kitchen to make breakfast before Katrina was fully awake. She wanted to make a good impression on her. Katrina could not go back to sleep when the aroma of lean bacon hit her nostrils. She just had to give in to the good smelling breakfast. When Katrina entered the kitchen, she found Jimmy and Nina wearing their robes waiting for her. Jimmy was reading the newspaper as he usually did every morning, and Lisa was drinking a glass of orange juice.

Katrina was trying her best to keep from limping due to the stab wound she received at the hands of Jean the night before. Jimmy was also surprised to learn in the paper that a prostitute listed by the name of Jean Murray was found dead in the back alley of a homeless shelter. According to the paper, an investigation was under way to find the murderer. The police mentioned the fact that there appeared to have been a struggle between Jean and her killer and that the killer could possibly be walking around with some wounds. Jimmy raised his head to look across at his mother while reading the paper, and she smiled at him. He was a little suspicious of her, but he shook it off when she got up to walk to the fridge to get some butter without showing any signs of pain.

They all sat at the table and ate breakfast, but Jimmy said very little to his mother. Katrina, however, was a little too talkative that morning. She was running her mouth a mile a minute, and most of what she was saying had nothing to do with anything. Her conversation went from how long Jimmy had known Lisa to how long Lisa had known Jimmy, information that she had heard from them the day before when she first came to the house. Jimmy's suspicions resurfaced and he knew that his mother might have had something to do with Jean's death. Getting it out of her would be a different story. It was easy for Jimmy to believe that his mother had murdered Jean, because he knew she was more than capable. She had killed before and right away she was under suspicion again.

Jimmy also acknowledged the fact that both times that Katrina had committed a crime; it was to protect her children from people who were trying to exploit them. It may have been a stupid move on Katrina's part, but Jimmy knew that he no longer had to worry about Jean exposing him. A tape of Jean committing sexual acts with johns in the back of cars and shooting drugs up her arms had also surfaced at the police station in Boston. It had a post office box listed in New Hampshire that would throw off the police department's investigation. An open case of a serial killer reigning terror on the prostitutes in the streets of Nashua, New Hampshire threw the cops in Boston for a loop. They wondered if the serial killer had finally made his way down to Boston wreaking havoc on the city.

The police did not know where to begin because all the clues that they had tied Jean's death to a serial killer who liked to videotape his prostitute victims in action prior to killing them. There was no trace of fingerprints. The police department in New Hampshire had received many tapes from the serial killer taunting them, showing the prostitutes and their johns before they're killed. The tape

227

with Jean on it was all too similar and the police somehow connected Jean's murder to the serial killer in New Hampshire.

The serial killer's ammo was to expose the johns while he disposed of the women who committed petty crimes and sold themselves for money on the streets, because they could never satisfy their hunger for the green paper. He was like a vigilante who took it upon himself to clean up the streets in the Northeast. It now appeared as though he was making his way down to Boston from New Hampshire. After reading that part of the story, Jimmy was thrown off course, and the thought of his mother killing Jean was completely gone from his mind. He was somewhat relieved of the thought that he had a repeat murderer under his roof, even though she was his mother. He wanted to believe that Jean was killed by somebody else.

Karen had also arrived from California for the big dinner, and Eddy went to pick her up. After he picked up Karen, he called Jimmy to see if he could swing by to see his favorite nephew to update him on his progress at his new job with the foundation. Realizing quickly that his mother was sitting across the table from him, Jimmy told Eddy that he was going to be busy, and that they could catch up on things the following day at the dinner. Jimmy did not want Eddy to know that Katrina was back until the dinner. He wanted to have his family in a dinner setting, so whatever animosity or grudge they had towards each other would be forgiven once and for all. Lisa was sworn into secrecy about the fact that Katrina was in Boston, as well.

Pastor Jacobs also called Jimmy early that morning to make sure that there was no suspicion about what took place the previous night with Katrina and Jean. He acted like he was checking on Jimmy and Lisa, and he made no mention of having seen Katrina. He asked Jimmy if he should bring anything for the dinner, and Jimmy told him that everything was all set to just bring his good heart. He meant that literally, because he didn't want Pastor Jacobs to have a heart attack when he saw Katrina. Pastor Jacobs also had to lie to his wife about leaving home in the middle of the night to go meet with Katrina. He told her that he had to go help one of the girls from the community center who was considering running away from home. He did not even bother mentioning the fact that he took one of her overcoats from the closet. She had so many of them, she did not even notice the one missing.

Feeling relieved that his problem had gone away; Jimmy was trying his best to keep Katrina's return to Boston a big secret for the dinner party. He wanted to pleasantly surprise his entire family with Katrina's presence. His family was finally going to be back together and Jimmy wanted to savor the moment. Meanwhile, Katrina tried her best to tend to her wounds without letting Jimmy know that she was responsible for Jean's death.

Before Dinner

The day of the planned dinner finally arrived and the scheduled time of six o'clock in the evening was fast approaching. Katrina and Lisa spent the whole day in the kitchen cooking together. Katrina's culinary skills had improved tremendously since she last saw her children. While in jail, her duties were shifted around a lot based on need. Katrina was an opportunist who looked for ways to improve her stay while in prison. During the third year of her sentence, Katrina realized that the inmates would go to great lengths to perform special favors for the cafeteria staff so they could have extra food. Katrina managed to have her duties shift from the laundry room to the cafeteria, and it was there that she learned how to make a few dishes.

While performing her duties in the kitchen, Katrina became the best student under the guidance of the head cook. She learned how make lasagna, potatoes au gratin, steak tips, and a few other dishes. For the dinner, Katrina wanted to make her favorite potatoes au gratin and lasagna. Lisa decided to make shrimp scampi, clam chowder, garlic bread, and her favorite dessert, chocolate soufflé. There was enough food on the table to feed a family of thirty. The ladies knew that they had done a great job with the food, and they could not wait to see the people's faces when they start eating.

After a long day in the kitchen, Lisa and Katrina spent a few moments relaxing in the game room located in the basement of the house. Katrina almost poured her heart out to her daughter-in-law. She told Lisa how she felt about neglecting her children, and that she had had a hard time dealing with the fact that she had allowed her weakness for drugs to control her life. Turning her back on Jimmy was especially hard, because he was her youngest child. Lisa told Katrina that Jimmy was more than happy to learn that she was alive, and in due time she knew that her husband would forgive his mother completely.

After relaxing in the game room for about an hour, the ladies returned to the living room to continue their little girl-on-girl talk. Katrina realized that Lisa was not just physically beautiful, but she was also a beautiful person inside and out. Lisa also realized how harsh a life that Katrina had led, and she was surprised that Katrina was even able to maintain her integrity to live on. The time that Lisa and Katrina spent together was very essential because all the bias that Lisa carried with her for Katrina was almost completely erased. She knew that her husband was lucky to have been born to a mother like Katrina.

Meanwhile, Jimmy was in the family room watching ESPN. He was listening to all the doubters who still believed that it was going to be too hard for him to ever come back and play, much less dominate on the basketball court like he once did. Since his mind was now free of worry, he wanted to concentrate on returning to basketball to prove his doubters, once again, how wrong they were about him. Jimmy's body responded well to the kidney, and he wanted to start playing pick-up games as soon as he could.

A Family Reunion

Everyone was dressed by 5:45 pm and Jimmy wanted his mother to stay in the guest room until after everyone arrived. Katrina was lying down in her bra and underwear on the bed anticipating seeing her parents again for the first time in over twenty-five years. She had forgotten what her younger brother Eddy and her younger sister Karen looked like. What she worried about most was the mean streak in her father that caused her departure from home when she was only fourteen years old. She wondered if he had changed at all or if he had gotten meaner over the years. She also felt bad for her mother who stayed because she didn't want to desert her family. Katrina was also overcome with joy, because she had made her way back into the lives of her children and now she also had grandchildren.

As Katrina lay on her back thinking about her long journey from the time she was fourteen to the present, tears started flowing down her cheeks. She knew that it was a long journey, and the only reason that she made it at all was because the Lord wanted to keep her around, so he performed a miracle. She got off the bed and knelt down on her knees and started praying and thanking the Lord for all that he had done for her. Katrina had never lost faith, and it was her faith that carried her through the years.

She could hear the doorbell ring as the people started to arrive one by one. Pastor Jacobs and his wife were the first people to arrive. Then it was Collin, Nina and their children. Katrina started getting dressed after Nina and her family arrived. Nina excused herself and signaled to Lisa that she wanted to go up to the bedroom to see

Katrina. She told her husband to watch the kids while she went upstairs to see Katrina.

Before she could reach the first step her son, Collin Jr., asked, "Is grandma gonna eat with us today?" Nina turned around and played it off, "Sure. Nana is on her way now." She said this as if she was she was talking about Katrina's mother, Mrs. Johnson. Collin Jr. then replied "Not Nana, our new Grandma!" Nina ran back towards Collin Jr. and whispered in his ear, "If you still want Mommy to get you ice scream, you need to stop telling people about grandma, ok?" He said, "Yes, Mommy!" Nina ran back towards the stairs to go find her mother.

Nina found Katrina standing in front of the mirror on the dresser looking at herself and smiling. She was wearing a light blue strapless dress and a light blue cardigan sweater. She asked Nina if her choice of dress was right. The big smile on Nina's face and the big nod she gave her mother took away all the doubts about the dress. This was actually the first time that Nina ever shared the experience of watching and helping her mother get dressed. The two women acted like two sisters who had never been apart. Katrina looked extremely good for her age, even though years on the street as a drug user had taken away some of her youth. The beautiful veneer implants she got in Phoenix brought back the beautiful smile she once had.

Nina could not believe how amazing her mother looked, and she knew that Pastor Jacobs' wife had better watched out because Katrina was about to have a whole new affect on her husband. After Nina helped with applying Katrina's make–up, she was ready to go downstairs and stun everyone. First, Nina had to talk to Jimmy about how they wanted to introduce their mother to the family. While

Jimmy and Nina were in the kitchen talking, the doorbell rang and it was Mr. and Mrs. Johnson, Karen, and Eddy. The last of the group had arrived and everyone was ushered into the formal dining where Lisa had set the table for thirteen people. Everyone took a seat at the dining room table, but there was still an empty seat left. Mr. and Mrs. Johnson asked why there was an extra seat at the table, and that is when Jimmy asked to have everyone's attention. He had a big announcement to make.

"First, I would like to thank everyone for being here today. Nina, Lisa, and I wanted to take this opportunity to invite everyone over to share in our joy of reconnecting with someone we all thought was taken from the family forever. It's not often that people are given a second chance in life, but as a family we have been given more than our share." At this point, everyone turned to look at Karen. It seemed as if Jimmy was referring to Karen in his speech, and everyone was ready to applaud. Before they could put their hands together, he told them that he was not done yet.

Jimmy continued, "I know that we agonized over the fact that aunty Karen was missing for years, and by the grace of God she was returned to us intact and we are grateful for that and want to celebrate her presence as well. But this time, God used his power in ways unimaginable to all of us. He has brought to us the final missing piece that links our family, a mother, a daughter, a sister, a grandmother, and an all-around wonderful woman. Ladies and gentlemen, please put your hands together and welcome my mother, Ms. Katrina Johnson, back to our family." Jimmy was eloquent in his introduction.

There was silence in the room across the table where Mr. and Mrs. Johnson, Collin, Karen, and Eddy were all sitting for about thirty seconds, because none of them could believe that Katrina was still alive Pastor Jacobs, Lisa, Jimmy, and Nina were clapping like they had just won the state lottery. Everything seemed like a miracle as Katrina appeared wearing her light blue dress with light blue stilettos; a nice pair of dangling platinum earrings, and a nice platinum charm bracelet courtesy of Jimmy. Mr. and Mrs. Johnson's jaws almost hit the table. Eddy could not contain himself as he ran towards Katrina, and lifted her off the ground in a bear hug. Karen joined her brother in hugging her sister, but Mrs. Johnson was too emotional and dumbfounded to move from her seat. She sat there idle with tears running down her face and smiling at the same time. Mr. Johnson was too embarrassed to say anything to his daughter. After Mrs. Johnson nudged him on his side, he got up and walked over to his daughter and told her how he had missed her and how sorry he was for acting so cruel when she was younger.

Katrina was taken back a little by her father's sudden change of heart. She didn't realize that Mr. Johnson had changed over time, and that her kids were able to bring life into an otherwise scorned man. Pastor Jacobs took notice of Katrina's beauty almost instantly as he walked over to hug her as if he had just seen her for the first time in over twenty something years. Katrina had transformed herself into the beautiful woman that she once was, and everyone was happy that she was still alive.

After hugging, kissing, and holding Katrina for close to thirty minutes it was time for Pastor Jacobs to say grace and bless the food. In between bites, Katrina would tell everyone the tales of her old life and her newfound one in Phoenix. She had a new zeal to live life and be the mother and grandmother that she had always wanted to be for her children and grandchildren. Mr. and Mrs. Johnson couldn't believe the inconceivable ways in which Katrina had to fight to survive while she was on the streets and in jail. Jimmy and Nina confirmed some of her detailed accounts about her battle with drugs and the neglect of her family. Katrina made sure that everyone knew that she was a better person, in a better place, and that the street life and drugs were a lesson that she had to learn in order for her to become the strong woman that she was.

There was so much that Katrina and her parents needed to catch up on. She had to call Candy in Phoenix to ask her for yet another week extension on her vacation. Candy was more than happy to honor her request. Everyone in the family was happy that Katrina was going to be spending an extra two weeks with them in Boston, and her time would be split among her children, grandchildren, her brother and sister, and her parents. Katrina was also happy to finally meet Collin, whom she thought was adorably handsome and extremely well-mannered.

Tying Up the Loose Ends

While the festivities were going on and everyone was celebrating the return of Katrina to her family, Katrina asked to speak with Pastor Jacobs in private. Mrs. Jacobs gave her husband an okay nod to go speak with Katrina in private. She was self-assured that her husband would never cross the line with another woman; even a woman who looked as fine as Katrina and who had given birth to his son.

Katrina wanted to speak to Pastor Jacobs for two reasons. The first reason being to thank him for looking after her children while she was absent from their lives. Jimmy and Nina had made it clear to Katrina that without the help and guidance of Pastor Jacobs they probably wouldn't have made it this far in life. For that, Katrina was grateful. She wanted to make sure that she expressed her gratitude to Pastor Jacobs for being a father to both of them. The second reason she wanted to talk to Pastor Jacobs was to ask him about what she should do with regard to Jean's murder. Katrina was very sorry for killing Jean, but she was in a situation where she was either going to kill or be killed. Katrina started to explain to Pastor Jacobs Jean and her aggression toward her during the confrontation, but Pastor Jacobs told her that he was already aware of the situation. She wanted to make sure he knew that she only went to talk to her to ask her to back off her son. While she was very remorseful about the murder, she didn't really want to go to the police. Pastor Jacobs reassured Katrina and told her not to worry because he had taken care of everything.

During the past few months he serial killer who had been killing prostitutes on the streets of Nashua, New

Hampshire had dominated the news headlines from Lowell to Boston and every town in between around the New England area. The total count of his victims had amounted to nine. As a cautionary measure, the police department and the media alerted the public. Pastor Jacobs was an avid newspaper reader and a well-informed person. He read the Boston Herald, Boston Globe and the New York Times daily. He had been following the murder spree in the paper and he figured out the ammo that the killer had been using. Initially, he wanted to use the footage of Jean on camera to try to negotiate with her and if she refused his deal, he was going to send the tape to the police station. However, his plans to use the footage changed when Katrina became entangled in the murder.

Pastor Jacobs told Katrina that he decided instead to use the captured footage of Jean on camera to help derail the police in their investigation, so that she's not found out. Pastor Jacobs was well aware of the steps that Katrina had taken to change her life and he knew that she was far more valuable to the teenagers in her program in Phoenix than she would have been behind bars. Armed with the knowledge of the pattern of the killer, he knew that the police would blame this new murder on the existing killer and Katrina would be able to walk away without getting caught. There was nothing left at the scene to tie Katrina to Jean's death and Pastor Jacobs got rid of the evidence that he found in Katrina's car.

After he detailed the car himself, he drove it to the parking lot of the church where Katrina could pick it up. She hadn't told him about the excuse she used to explain to Jimmy why she didn't drive herself back home on the night of the murder, so he asked her to repeat everything to him so he could be informed. She told him that she told

Jimmy that she was too tired to drive herself home that night and that she left the car over her friend's house and that she would pick up the car when she was ready. Pastor Jacobs thought it was a good enough excuse as he made plans to pick her up the next day to go pick up the rental car.

Katrina was still a little nervous about the witness who told the cops that she saw an old woman running from the scene. But Pastor Jacobs assured her that the police would think that the killer used a disguise to throw them off and their search would be for a male serial killer. Pastor Jacobs told Katrina that prayer would do her a lot of good and only God could forgive her for taking someone else's life. The two of them had been in the room for close to fifteen minutes and Pastor Jacobs knew it was a matter of time before his wife came looking for him. He wanted to wrap things up and made sure that Katrina knew what time he was going to pick her up the next day to get the rental car.

Know When To Let It Slide

As Pastor Jacobs and Katrina made their way out of the room, they could hear the toilet being flushed in the bathroom. It was Collin, he had gotten up to use the bathroom and while he was in the bathroom he couldn't keep from eavesdropping on Pastor Jacob and Katrina's conversation. He heard their whole conversation and was in a position as a police lieutenant to make an arrest and solve a murder that he would be highly recognized for. Collin found himself once again in the midst of a confession to a killing by a member of his wife's family. But this time, he had to fight his conscience for but a few seconds to decide that he wasn't going to do anything about it.

Collin thought about the way the Boston Police department treated his wife and the way they forced her out of a job and he came to the conclusion that the crime was committed out of his area and therefore out of his hands. Arresting a woman who was defending herself against an attacker wasn't going to do anything, but add to the stereotype that black people are savages who kill at will no matter what the situation. Collin also realized that the life of a white prostitute was probably going to be downplayed in the media as someone who was struggling to make it in society instead of the criminal that she really was.

At the end of the day, it was going to be one more strike against the black race and Collin didn't want to add to the daily grief of black folks in the ghetto. He walked back to the living room without saying anything to Katrina or Pastor Jacobs. However, Katrina and Pastor Jacobs had good enough sense to know that Katrina should go back to Phoenix the following day until the Boston Police Department came to a conclusion for Jean's murder.

A Sudden Change of Heart

Pastor Jacobs drove to Jimmy's house the next day to pick up Katrina so she could pick up the rental car from the church parking lot. Luckily Katrina had parked the car away from the alley, because the witness didn't where she fled to. Jimmy and Lisa had gone out to run a few errands, so they weren't there to see her leave. When Pastor Jacobs pulled up in front of the house, he found Katrina waiting with her bags packed and ready to leave town. It was hard for Katrina to depart so suddenly, but it was something that had to be done. Pastor Jacobs popped open his trunk and got out of his car to help Katrina with her luggage. Katrina was very sad as Pastor Jacobs peeled out of Jimmy's driveway to head to his church.

She cried silently in the car and wondered why everything always went so wrong whenever she was around her children. Pastor Jacobs simply told her "there's a reason for everything that happens in life and sometimes people have to let go of the big expectations in order to savor the small moments in life." Katrina wanted so much to stay in Boston for an extra couple of weeks to get to know her family, but at the risk of being arrested for Jean's murder, she made the wise decision to leave.

Pastor Jacobs told her how great it was to see her again as he loaded her baggage in the trunk of her car after he arrived at the church parking lot. He gave her a long hug and a kiss on the cheek as he wiped the tears from her yes. He assured Katrina that the whole family would come to Phoenix as soon as they could to spend time with her and they would be looking forward to meeting Candy, the woman, who helped her get her life together.

Katrina drove straight to the airport to catch her flight to Phoenix, Arizona. After boarding the plane, while Katrina was sitting in her seat waiting for the plane to take off, she called Jimmy's house and left him a message. She started "I know that I'm looking like a bad mother to you again, but situations beyond my control have forced me do leave you so suddenly. I wish that I could explain to you in more detail why I had to go, but I can't. Just know that I love you and your sister very much and your spouses and that I will be looking forward to seeing you guys in Phoenix very soon."

Never Say Goodbye

Just as Jimmy started to play the message that Katrina left for him, he turned on the television and the police chief was talking about Jean's death and the possibility that there could've been a copycat killer. Jimmy knew then what his mother had done and it was a sacrifice that he was more than grateful for. He knew that if his mother had extended her stay in Boston, there was a possibility that she could've been tied to the murder and he would have to go without her for another twenty-five years of his life. Knowing that she was just an airplane flight away from him was satisfying enough. He never wanted to say goodbye to her because he knew that he would see her again very soon.

Although Nina didn't get a message from Katrina, Jimmy was able to convince her and his grandparents that Katrina was needed in Phoenix and she had to leave abruptly due to an emergency. Nina was a little sad that she didn't spend much time with her mother, but Katrina left a good enough impression on her heart that would last until the next time they saw each other.

Katrina went to Boston and discovered a new family that was very different from the one she left behind when she went to jail. Her father had changed, her mother was happy, her brother and sister were responsible adults and her children were successful beyond her dreams. She realized that she had asked God for a lot in her life, but she never thought that he would deliver so much. Katrina was happy that she didn't say goodbye to her family because she knew that they would be with her in Phoenix and took with her the memories of a wonderfully happy family.

She was even happier when the whole family showed up in Phoenix six weeks later for a surprised visit. Everyone stayed at her house and some people slept on the floor reminiscent of when she was a child. Back then, she had to give up her bed and sleep on the floor with her siblings when her grandparents, aunts and uncles came to visit in Boston. She didn't mind doing it this time for her children, grandchildren, brother, sister and her parents. It was the beginning of the Johnson family becoming a tight knit family for the first time.

Stay tuned for the very first part of this trilogy.

Ignorant Souls

(The Prequel)

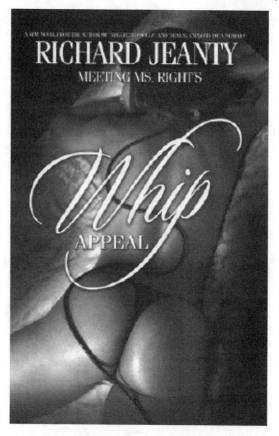

Malcolm is a wealthy virgin who decides to conceal his wealth
From the world until he meets the right woman. His wealthy best
friend, Dexter, hides his wealth from no one. Malcolm struggles to find
love in an environment where vanity and materialism are rampant,
while Dexter is getting more than enough of his share of women.
Malcolm needs develop self-esteem and confidence to meet the right
woman and Dexter's confidence is borderline arrogance.

Will bad boys like Dexter continue to take women for a ride?

Or Will nice guys like Malcolm continue to finish last?

Tina develops an insatiable sexual appetite very early in life. She only loves her boyfriend, Darren, but he's too far away in college to satisfy her sexual needs.

Tina decides to get buck wild away in college
Will her sexual trysts jeopardize the lives of the men in her life?

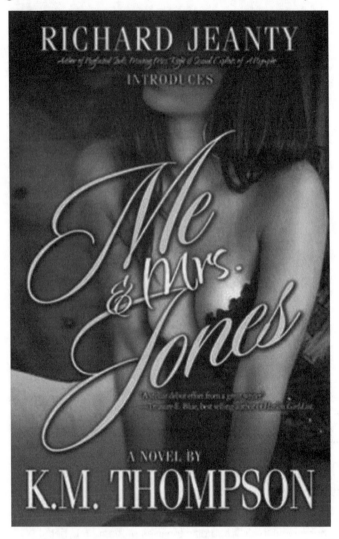

Faith Jones, a woman in her mid-thirties, has given up on ever finding love again until she met her son's best friend, Darius. Faith Jones is walking a thin line of betrayal against her son for the love of Darius. Will Faith allow her emotions to outweigh her common sense?

Richard Jeanty

Motherhood and the trials of loving too hard and not enough frame
this story...The realism of these characters will bring tears to your
spirit as you discover the hero in the villain you never saw coming...
Neglected Souls is a gritty, honest and heart stirring story of hope
and personal triumph set in the ghettos of Boston.

Betrayal, lust, lies, murder, deception, sex and tainted love frame this story... Julian Stevens lacks the ambition and freak ability that Miko looks for in a man, but she married him despite his flaws to spite an ex-boyfriend. When Miko least expects it, the old boyfriend shows up and ready to sweep her off her feet again. Suddenly the grass grows greener on the other side, but Miko is not an easily satisfied woman. She wants her cake and eat it too. While Miko's doing her own thing, Julian is determined to become everything Miko ever wanted in a man and more, but will he go to extreme lengths to prove he's worthy of Miko's love? Julian Stevens soon finds out that he's capable of being more than he could ever imagine as he embarks on a journey that will change his life forever.

Order these exciting novels from

RJ Publications

Available at bookstores everywhere.

Use this coupon to order by mail.

❑ NEGLECTED SOULS (0976053454 – $14.95)
❑ MEETING MS. RIGHT'S WHIP APPEAL (0976927705 – $14.95)
❑ SEXUAL EXPLOITS OF A NYMPHO (0976927721 – $14.95)
❑ ME AND MRS. JONES (097692773X – 14.95)

Name _____
Address _____
City _____ State _____ Zip Code _____

Please send me the novels I have checked above.

Free Shipping and Handling

Total Number of Books _____

Total Amount Due _____

This offer subject to change without notice.

Send check or money order (no cash or CODs) to:

RJ Publications
842 S. 18th Street, Suite 3
Newark, NJ 07108

For more information call 973-373-2445, or visit www.rjpublications.com.
Please allow 2 – 3 weeks for delivery.

Neglected No More

A novel

By

Richard Jeanty

RJ Publications, LLC

Newark, New Jersey

FRANKLIN BRANCH LIBRARY

13651 E. MCNICHOLS RD.

DETROIT, MI 48205

MAR   2010

DAMAGE NOTED FR

Neglected No More   Richard Jeanty

The characters and events in this book are fictitious. Any resemblance to actual persons, living or dead, is purely coincidental.

RJ Publications
rjeantay@yahoo.com
www.rjpublications.com
Copyright © 2006 by Richard Jeanty
All Rights Reserved
ISBN 0-9769277-4-8

Without limiting the rights under copyright reserved above, no part of this book may be reproduced in any form whatsoever without the prior consent of both the copyright owner and the above publisher of this book.

Printed in Canada

October 2006

11 12 13 14 15 16 17 18 19 20

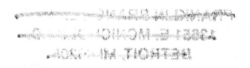